*Maryland Loyalists
in the American Revolution*

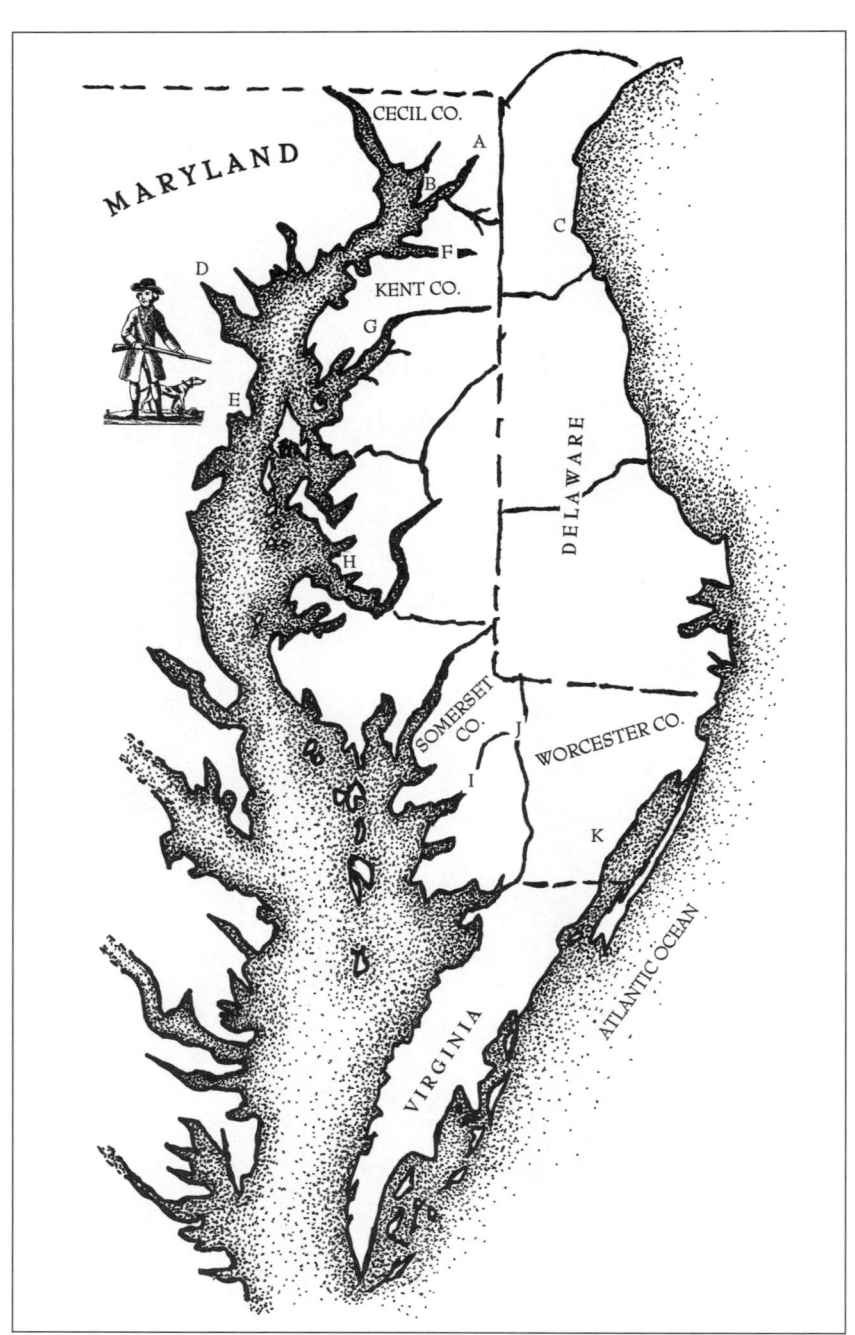

Maryland Loyalists
in the American Revolution

By M. Christopher New

Tidewater Publishers
Centreville, Maryland

Copyright © 1996 by Tidewater Publishers

All rights reserved. No part of this book may be used or reproduced in any manner whatsoever without written permission except in the case of brief quotations embodied in critical articles or reviews. For information, address Tidewater Publishers, Centreville, Maryland 21617.

Library of Congress Cataloging-in-Publication Data

New, M. Christopher, 1961–
   Maryland loyalists in the American Revolution / by M. Christopher New. — 1st ed.
      p.   cm.
   Includes bibliographical references and index.
   ISBN 0-87033-495-6 (hardcover)
    1. American loyalists—Maryland.   2. Maryland—History—Revolution, 1775–1783.   I. Title.
E277.N49 1996
973.3'14—dc21   96–47702
                                                                                      CIP

Manufactured in the United States of America
First edition

For my wife and my parents
(and everyone else who puts up with me)

I DO hereby Certify, That   has, in my Prefence, voluntarily taken an OATH, to bear Faith and true Allegiance to His MAJESTY KING GEORGE the Third; --and to defend to the utmoft of his Power, His facred Perfon, Crown and Government, against all Perfons whatfoever.

GIVEN under my Hand at   this   Day of
In the Seventeenth Year of His MAJESTY'S Reign, Anno. Dom. 1777.

Contents

Preface	ix
1. Countdown to Revolution	3
2. James Chalmers and Plain Truth	18
3. Conflict	35
4. Royal Provincials	52
5. A Cunning Plan	66
6. Fighting the Spanish	81
7. Exiles	99
8. Strange Days	115
Appendix	133
Notes	163
Bibliography	173
Index	181

Preface

Someone once said to me that the American Revolution is unconsciously taught as holy scripture. To bolster his theory, he cited George Washington, John Hancock, and Samuel Adams as the Revolutionary equivalent of the Trinity, with Benedict Arnold filling in as Judas and a special guest appearance by King George III as Pontius Pilate.

As provocative as that theory may be, I prefer to view American thought on the revolution as a larger-than-life folktale. Good folklore is an exaggeration of reality. There's a comfortable, recognizable formula which is always at work: Good guys are really good; bad guys are really bad. It's a black-and-white world with absolutely no shades of gray. Unfortunately, when we deal with real people doing real things, reality is often nothing *but* shades of gray. Good people sometimes do bad things and vice versa.

In the process of compressing the American Revolution into the history textbooks between the Plymouth Pilgrims and the War of 1812, the subject of loyalists has always fallen through the cracks. Several excellent books on loyalists have appeared but their impact on the folktale has been light. Who has time for traitors? We need to hear the story about Washington never telling a lie, which, of course, is a fabrication. Keeping a ragtag army together against all odds *and* winning the war wasn't quite good enough for the school kiddies, thought people in the nineteenth century. It suited the Victorian mind to throw in silly folklore and make Washington so lofty that the real man utterly disappeared.

Like more than a few generations of Americans, I went through school thinking we won the American Revolution because we cleverly hid behind rocks and killed redcoats who were stupid enough to stand out in the open, their uniforms making them easy targets. America good, England bad—a simple message driven home by Americans because they won the war and were going to make themselves feel good about it.

The poor British soldiers! Redcoats are essentially eighteenth-century Nazis in our collective unconscious. Oddly enough, even the Brits don't seem to have a much better view of them. Opponents of the war in the British Parliament were known to publicly glory in English defeats, and no battle honors were handed out to British officers serving in the North American campaign. Ironically, American writers have actually written the more sympathetic comments on redcoats.

For many years, I have observed very closely how people react to the subject of loyalists. Any mention of the word "loyalist" usually elicits a blank stare—there is nothing in the general public's mental database to help them understand. Say the word "tory," however, and there is instant recognition. First, there's the smirk, followed by the inevitable "Oh, the bad guys!"

This mind-set creates all sorts of problems for the well-meaning historian. Some become so annoyed at the common prejudice against loyalists that they immediately place them on a pedestal, creating a combination martyr and superhero. I hope I have not fallen into that particular trap.

In the case of the Maryland Loyalist Regiment, we have a group of people who lost everything. They encountered bad luck at every turn. Disease, death, desertion, shipwreck—you name it, they faced it. The result was perhaps something they never could have anticipated: Their very existence became the smallest possible footnote in the war. What's more, anyone alive at the time probably would have been surprised at their eventual slip into obscurity. The regiment's senior officers continually came in contact with the most important British leaders in the military campaign. Bad timing or bad luck always landed the regiment in the worst circumstances, despite the best efforts of its lieutenant colonel to make the regiment a formidable presence.

James Chalmers of Kent County, Maryland, was an articulate commander who published a well-known loyalist pamphlet and struggled for influence with the British high command. He corresponded with the likes of William Franklin, the loyalist son of Benjamin Franklin; John André (General Charles "No Flint" Grey's aide-de-camp), who would later be hanged as a spy by George Washington in the aftermath of Benedict Arnold's treason; Adjutant General Lord Rawdon; and General Sir William Howe, commander of British forces in America.

Teenage ensign William Augustus Bowles of Frederick would become a powerful foe of the United States as the defiant director general of the Creek Indian Nation after the war—so powerful a foe that President Thomas Jefferson came close to committing a military force to recapture a fort that Bowles had seized with his Indians.

Some from the loyalist regiment would turn their lives around completely. Captain Philip Barton Key, the uncle of Francis Scott Key, became a loyalist in opposition to his brother John, who served as a patriot officer. Philip Barton Key's life after the war brings new meaning to the word "irony." He returned to Annapolis and started a law practice with great success. Later, he served the defense in the first great legal battle to rattle the federal government: the impeachment proceedings against Supreme Court Justice Samuel Chase who, twenty-eight years before, had signed the Declaration of Independence as part of Maryland's delegation. Despite some mudslinging from opponents concerning his loyalist past, Philip Barton Key was elected to Congress in 1806. His constituency must have been very forgiving—or very forgetful.

The Maryland Loyalist Regiment itself seldom saw action in the conflict, thanks to British superiors who considered loyalists useful for emptying chamber pots and not much else. When the unit became involved in a fierce battle at Pensacola against the Spanish, the loyal Marylanders fought with distinction. The battle, however, was lost and the entire Florida campaign forgotten in the long shadow of larger battles like Bunker Hill and Saratoga.

In 1783, the Maryland Loyalists, if they had not died or deserted, had lost not only the war but also their homes and, frequently, had alienated themselves from members of their families who had joined the rebellion. As if that weren't enough, they were then shipped off to New Brunswick to start a new life in the Canadian wilderness. As they neared their new home, they were shipwrecked. These people simply did not have good luck on their side.

After two hundred years, the only loyalists who receive passing mention in the history books are those who committed colorful atrocities during the war. This, of course, makes for good reading—the literary equivalent of the movie car chase. Unfortunately, the average loyalist, a man who was faced with the most difficult decision of his life and its consequences, has been consigned to the cruelest fate of all: obscurity. As loyalist researcher Lorenzo Sabine observed in the preface to his groundbreaking *Loyalists of the American Revolution*, ". . . Such men leave few memorials behind them. Their papers are scattered and lost, and their very names pass from human recollection." These words were not written in the midst of the Bicentennial. Sabine wrote his observations in 1864, just a few decades after the last of the loyalists had died.

Whenever possible, I've tried to let people speak for themselves through direct quotes. Often the best way to experience what is happening to a particular person is to hear it from his or her mouth rather than through the clumsy paraphrasing of a writer more than two hundred years after the fact. The art of eighteenth-century spelling has been left intact except where I felt it became confusing to the modern reader.

Some may be put off by the idea of calling our founding fathers "rebels," a term that occurs often in the text. It is very misleading to call them Americans, because the loyalists were also Americans (the term "American" in reference to British colonists in North America predates the eighteenth century). Even calling them "patriots" seems a bit, well, patronizing. Therefore, they are frequently called what the British called them: rebels. Since they were rebelling against the ruling government, the term is justifiable. General Washington, please accept my apologies.

As I researched materials for this book, I often came across fragments of Maryland loyalist information buried in the footnotes of research articles. More than one of the authors expressed geniune surprise that no one had ever written a comprehensive study on Maryland loyalists. This work is meant to provide that missing link.

Maryland Loyalists in the American Revolution endeavors to blow the dust off some rather interesting people—real people who were often pillars of their communities but whose names have vanished from the history of their towns as if they had never existed. Some of them were good, some were bad. Nevertheless, they are all equal now.

It is, of course, impossible to do this kind of work without the help of those unsung heroes: librarians and researchers. I am indebted to all those who helped me fill in so many pieces of a puzzle that will probably never be completed. In particular, thanks must go to researchers Martin Lubowski in London, England, and Don Dixon of Fredericton, New Brunswick; Sandra Johnson, the curator/director of the Pensacola Historical Society; Eileen M. Clarke of the United Empire Loyalists' Association; Evelyn Costello of the Saint John Regional Library in Saint John, New Brunswick; Scott Staton; Hector Diaz; Ron Cash; and Chris Ward. Thanks also to the British Museum Library for furnishing James Chalmers's 1796 *Strictures* pamphlet.

The good folks at many libraries deserve mention: the William L. Clements Library at the University of Michigan; Kathryn Hilder and the Harriet Irving Library at the University of New Brunswick; the amazing David Library of the American Revolution at Washington's Crossing, Pennsylvania; Ernest L. Scott Jr. and the Maryland Historical Society in Baltimore.

To those I have overlooked, a sincere "thank you" must suffice.

In this book, Maryland *Loyalists* are members of the Maryland Loyalist Regiment and Maryland *loyalists* are all those who supported the cause.

*Maryland Loyalists
in the American Revolution*

Countdown to Revolution

The true history of the American Revolution can never be written.... A great many people in those days were not at all what they seemed, nor what they are generally believed to have been.

—John Jay
PRESIDENT OF THE CONTINENTAL CONGRESS,
FIRST CHIEF JUSTICE OF THE UNITED STATES

A NEW LAND

It may have started with the first Englishman who stood upon the shores of the New World in the early 1600s. He strolled back and forth on the virgin beaches, staring with apprehension at the dense, forbidding forest beyond. Then it dawned on him: He was completely and utterly alone. Everything he knew was thousands of miles away. All of the elements that made up his culture, the things that made him English, now existed only in his head. Unloading the boats, the Englishman and his fellow settlers began to build their new version of England. Many elements remained the same; many, however, mutated and became uniquely American.

Generation after generation followed. As the years passed, the number of native-born colonists began to outnumber those arriving by ship. Fewer and fewer had actually seen England. "King and country" became a vague phrase, still spoken but losing its emotional meaning. The psychological distance between England and the colonies grew. At first, the change was slight—almost imperceptible. The colonists began to speak differently, a fact noted as early as 1735 when a traveler mentioned the use of "barbarous English" by colonists in the south.[1]

As the 1700s progressed, some colonists still thought of themselves as Englishmen. Others were quick to see themselves as something different, something apart from England. Thus, the seeds of revolution were planted and the liberty tree grew quickly. The English would eventually try to prune it, only to discover they had waited far too long.

Maryland, "The Eccentrick Colony"

In 1632, King Charles I of England granted to George Calvert, Lord Baron of Baltimore, a great section of land north of the Potomac River in the new world. In honor of the king's wife, Henrietta Maria (Mary), the new colony was to be called Maryland. In the charter, the land was owned by a single person, called the proprietary, who appointed the governor and other officers.

This was a different arrangement from the other emerging colonies, where affairs were either controlled by the king of England or by governors and other officers elected by the people. The Maryland charter created, for all intents and purposes, an empire within an empire.

And Maryland geography created, in effect, two separate colonies. To the west of the Bay were St. Mary's City, Annapolis, and the tiny Baltimore Town. The inhabitants were in constant contact with travelers from the north and south. On the Eastern Shore, however, the inhabitants were nearly isolated from outside influences. This would soon cause problems.

These early years were indeed turbulent. Territorial disputes with the Virginians were waged for years. The relationship with the neighboring Indians was generally friendly except for the Susquehannocks and Nanticokes, who occasionally burned houses and murdered settlers.

More dilemmas were soon at hand. Lord Baltimore's charter was opposed, civil war erupted in England, and a rebellion of Puritans against the proprietary government nearly resulted in the ruin of the young colony.

The unique character of Maryland government changed when William and Mary came to the throne of England. In 1691, the king commissioned the first royal governor of Maryland and the colony became subject to the control of the monarchy. One of the first results of the new government was subordination of Catholics. Originally intended as a refuge for Catholics, Maryland now harbored an attitude as intolerant as that of the mother country toward "papists." The Church of England became firmly established and prayers for the king were part of every Anglican service.

Throughout the 1700s, an independent spirit began to emerge in the Maryland colony. During the French and Indian War of the 1750s, when England and France clashed over possession of the northern colonies, Governor Horatio Sharpe fought with the lower house of the assembly, whose members believed the proprietary should contribute to the defense of the province by paying taxes on his estates. Sharpe wasn't keen on this idea but had little choice except to yield to their demands.

When the English won the war, they probably didn't realize they had established an environment in which rebellion could flourish. Now that the colonists were free from the threat of French incursions from Canada, they didn't really need England anymore.

The anger among the colonists arose when George III came to the throne and tried to bring the colonies back under the control of the monarchy. Taxes and protests were soon part of the landscape. In Maryland, the role of the monarchical system was questioned as well.

Antilon and *First Citizen*

On January 7, 1773, a commentary in support of policies of the proprietary government appeared in the Maryland Gazette under the name of "Antilon." This letter sparked a barbed response signed "First Citizen," and over the next six months, a series of letters between the two became well known in Maryland.

The identity of the writers was apparently quite obvious from the start. Antilon was the pen name of Daniel Dulany, Jr., an eminent lawyer who was considered to be one of the most distinguished men of his time. In the years before the Revolution, Dulany the younger held the offices of secretary and attorney-general of Maryland and was a member of the Maryland council. He was unquestionably a loyalist yet offered one of the most eloquent and defiant statements uttered against England.

In 1765, England had imposed the Stamp Act to offset the enormous costs of maintaining military protection of the colonies. The tax, the first direct tax Parliament imposed on the colony, affected most types of printed material: newspapers, broadsides, pamphlets, legal documents, even playing cards and dice.

When the colonists heard of this tax, they hit the ceiling. Their first strategy of avoiding it—they said they couldn't afford to pay—wasn't terribly effective. When that didn't work, the very handy phrase, "No taxation without representation," was suddenly bandied about. It was an instant hit with its target audience and the colonists would keep it as part of their propaganda campaign until independence was declared. Not content merely to talk defiance, the colonists soon had a movement afoot to boycott British goods.

In the midst of the colonial discontent, Dulany published *Considerations on the Propriety of Imposing Taxes in the British Colonies*. His pride in America was flaunted before his English "betters" as he said:

> A garment of linsey-woolsey [coarse fabric of domestic manufacture] when made the distinction of patriotism, is more honourable than the plumes and the diadem of an emperor, without it. Let the manufacture of America be the symbol of dignity and the badge of virtue, and it will soon break the fetters of distress.[2]

There were plenty of colonists, though, who took this kind of defiance as a cue to dismantle the whole system. Loyalists, to their shock and surprise, had let the cat out of the bag and were powerless to get it back in. Dulany's opposing correspondent was to lead the attack in Maryland politics.

Assuming the name "First Citizen," Charles Carroll was part of a wealthy Maryland Catholic family which was not on good terms with the Dulanys. Fifteen years younger than Dulany, Carroll was still unknown in politics largely because his Catholic faith barred him by law from public life. His exposure through the First Citizen letters would soon change all that.

These letters, although quite well known in their time, are a bit of a problem for the modern reader. For all their importance as a flashpoint in the Revolution, the letters now inspire mostly yawns. The main reason is that they involve very specific legislative practices that were on the minds of everyone in Annapolis in 1773 but which have long since been forgotten. Not helping matters is the frequent use of Latin phrases and references to things that have lost their meaning or impact over time.

The Letters

The political catfight between Dulany and Carroll started in an unspectacular way. In 1770, Robert Eden, Maryland's proprietary governor, issued a proclamation that established officers' fees based on a statute from 1763 which had lapsed because the upper and lower houses couldn't see eye to eye on a new tobacco inspection bill with a fee scale. The governor had hoped his actions would prevent "oppressions and extortions" by the officers.[3]

Dulany, a member of the upper house and advisor of the governor, believed that Eden was simply doing his job when the assembly failed to. In what can be recognized as a classic loyalist trait, he was a friend of established government. He didn't believe government was broken and certainly didn't think it needed fixing.

Enter Charles Carroll. His mistrust of England was nothing new. In 1760, after twelve years of study and travel abroad, Carroll wrote from London saying, "Our dear-bought liberty stands upon the brink of destruction." Two years later, he was back in Maryland and very convinced that the English Constitution was "hastening to its final period of dissolution, and the symptoms of a general decay are but too visible."[4]

Carroll was absolutely opposed to Eden's proclamation, sensing a trend toward government operating independently of the people. Unlike Dulany, he wasn't afraid of change. Government was constantly evolving, altered by each generation for the betterment of the people.

Dulany staunchly defended established government. Popular leaders who espoused new ideas were espousing anarchy. It could be argued his views were an extreme brand of conservatism. To members of the old school like Dulany, the English constitution was perfection, not something that needed improving by colonists.

In the first letter to the *Maryland Gazette*, Dulany composed a conversation between two characters named "First Citizen" and "Second Citizen," the latter his mouthpiece. A month later, Carroll submitted a letter under the name First Citizen saying that Antilon had misrepresented the viewpoints of First Citizen. Dulany was taken aback, not expecting any attack. He wrote three more letters to Carroll, who responded in turn. They fought each other on the meaning and implications of the English constitution, citing somewhat tedious examples to reinforce their points.

Each was more than happy to attack the character of the other. Some of the more interesting personal exchanges include:

> *Antilon:* "I am no rover." Indeed, Mr. First Citizen, I don't believe you are, any more than I believe you to be a man of honour, or veracity.
> *First Citizen (Concerning Antilon's arguments)*: But let us leave fiction, and come to reality.
> *Antilon (On First Citizen's professed knowledge of Antilon)*: "You knew me of old." Indeed. Pray, when did our acquaintance begin, how has it been improved into knowledge? Perhaps your knowledge has been gathered in your flights, when you was gifted with the powers of Ariel. Hard it is upon a poor mortal to encounter such supernatural intelligences.
> *First Citizen (regarding Antilon's writing style):* What a flow of words! How pregnant with thought and deep reason!
> *Antilon:* The many instances, in which you have shown your utter disregard of truth in your assertions and of the most disingenuous prevarication in your answers, and explications, render your testimony extremely suspicious.
> *First Citizen:* Antilon has not endeavoured to convince the minds of his readers by the force of reason.
> *Antilon:* My advice to you is to be quiet.
> *First Citizen:* Sleep in peace, good Antilon, if thy conscience will permit thee.

When the smoke cleared, one thing was clear. Dulany, a stickler for the old ways, was losing influence fast among restless Marylanders. Carroll had won the hearts of the *Gazette*'s readers with his arguments. He would carry the future with him—and add his signature to the Declaration of Independence.

Praise the Lord and Pass the Ammunition

By the summer of 1775, the British Army and the colonists had clashed at Lexington, Concord, and Bunker Hill. It was readily apparent to the colonists that they had turned down a road from which there was no return. Each colony set up committees to recruit militias and watch over the activities of potential loyalists.

In Maryland, most of the loyalists were on the Eastern Shore. These plantation owners, dirt farmers, and fishermen were encouraged to remain loyal in virtually every case by the local pastor.

Of all the potential enemies of the reformers, it was these men of the cloth who were perhaps the most dangerous. No class of citizens was as scrutinized, spied on, and threatened as the Anglican and Episcopalian ministers who remained loyal to the king. This loyalty ranged from refusing to omit the king's name from the service to demanding that the congregation actively resist the rebel movement. Their dedication to the status quo wasn't surprising considering that an Anglican clergyman at his ordination took an oath of loyalty to the king. In addition, prayers for the royal family were part of the Anglican ritual. Thus, it became rather difficult to remain Anglican, fight against England, and ask God to bless King George.

A colonist's faith frequently showed his political views. The Congregationalists of New England were patriots with very few exceptions, while Anglicans were mostly loyalist in their views. Generalizations, of course, can be dangerous. As loyalist historian Wallace Brown pointed out in his book *The Good Americans,* the Anglican Church boasted more signers of the Declaration of Independence than any other religion.

What rattled the patriot leaders was the power that the loyalist preachers wielded from their pulpits. Every week, a minister had a captive audience, most of whom viewed their spiritual leader with great respect. And the local reverend tried to make loyalty to the king seem like it had God's seal of approval. The patriots couldn't let this sort of thing go on.

In Maryland, especially, the revolutionaries had their hands full. As the pastor of the Chester parish in Chestertown, The Reverend John

Paterson was high on the list of tories to be silenced. His outspoken views quickly landed him in front of the Kent County Committee on August 21, 1775, to answer for his criticism of the actions of the committee. The reverend took the opportunity to declare that the committee and the Continental Congress were depriving men of their liberty. After calling the proceedings a mock trial, he concluded by saying "there was more liberty in *Turkey* than in this Province."[5]

In the course of being questioned, Paterson admitted his approval of Doctors Cooper and Chandler. Myles Cooper and Thomas Chandler were New York Anglican clergymen who had worked quite actively to create a unified Episcopal party against rebellion. Some time after the Boston Tea Party, Cooper went to Annapolis to discuss the current troubles with Reverend Jonathan Boucher at his rectory. The two then went to Philadelphia to attempt to build a coalition of Anglican clergymen to dissuade rebellion against the Crown. The attempt failed because some of the clergy were whigs and others merely wanted to remain neutral.

Originally from Virginia, The Reverend Boucher was a prolific writer, speaker, and teacher in his day, having at one time tutored George Washington's stepson. He was also a devout loyalist. In 1773, he had complained to another clergyman: "How often, how long shall I grumble & complain of the Strange Inattention of the Mother Country to these Countries! Without seeing, or, at least, without attending to it, She is suffering a strange refractory Spirit to grow up, which, ere long, will work her irremediable Woe."[6]

By 1775, that irremediable woe was all too evident. That year, Boucher delivered a sermon entitled "On Civil Liberty, Passive Obedience, and Nonresistance" to his flock at Queen Anne's parish. He found it impossible, however, to publish his views. Fortunately for historians, Boucher held on to his writings and published this sermon, considered by loyalist historians a classic essay of loyalist thought, after the war.

His arguments, not surprisingly, concern religion and how it relates to man's obedience to established authority. Boucher believed "obedience to government is every man's duty because it is every man's interest." He thought this was particularly important to Christians because "it is enjoined by the positive commands of God."[7]

Many notions becoming popular in revolutionary thought were frowned upon by Boucher. One of these was the idea that humans are equal, with no one being naturally inferior or subject to another's authority except by his own consent. Boucher found this to be "ill-founded and false both in its premises and conclusions. Every society requires a government and having a government requires some degree of 'inferiority and superiority.' " In essence, government requires governing people, and governing people requires that the people can't always do whatever crosses their minds.

Boucher saw obedience as total—the only thing a good Christian should do. He also believed that the spirit of rebellion would ruin any government put in place of the king's authority. The new government would fall as soon as the initial excitement wore off and discontent grew. Then the following government would suffer the same fate and so on and so on. In a religious context, Boucher thought this kind of social upheaval was immoral. Further, he was offended by churches where "they openly teach & inculcate Principles subversive of all good Government."[8]

With views like these, Boucher couldn't possibly continue in his position for long. Finally, after preaching for six months with two loaded pistols within easy reach on his pulpit cushion, the reverend left Maryland and sailed for London.

Other loyalist clergy had equal difficulties but managed to remain in Maryland. The Reverend John Bowie, rector of St. Martin's in Worcester County, refused to take the oath of fidelity. In a bit of high drama, Bowie declared he would "suffer his right arm to be cut off, and wished if he took it [the oath] his tongue might cling to the roof of his mouth and never come loose."[9] He was imprisoned in Annapolis but must have succeeded in keeping his views to himself because he was soon released. He returned to serve in several churches on the Eastern Shore.

The Reverend John Scott, also of Worcester, was investigated by the Maryland Council of Safety for similar tory views. After paying an enormous bond of one thousand pounds to be set free, he was not allowed to correspond or speak on public affairs.[10]

Others, like Boucher, would choose not to stay. In 1774, The Reverend William Edmondston of Cecil County reacted to the calls for collecting arms and ammunition by circulating pamphlets which asked that the people continue their allegiance to the British government. Naturally, this didn't sit well with the rebel movement and he was hauled before a committee and required to sign a paper recanting everything he had said. When he refused, he was eventually threatened with having his house torn down if he didn't sign. The situation grew intolerable and Edmondston left for England with his wife and family in November 1775.[11] One of his Cecil County neighbors would soon experience a similar crisis.

The Continental Congressman

Robert Alexander was an important and influential Marylander in 1775. Born and raised in Cecil County, he owned a large farm which was located in the area known as Head of Elk (present-day Elkton).

Alexander had been associated with the colonists' cause for some time before the war. When Boston harbor was closed by the British in the aftermath of the Boston Tea Party, the colonies agreed to stop all imports from Great Britain. When Baltimore got the news of this proposal, it set up a committee of correspondence to chart the progress of events and keep in touch with the other colonies. Robert Alexander was the first person elected to the committee. Consequently, he was closely involved in local matters, rubbing shoulders with the likes of Charles Ridgely, Thomas Cockey, and Matthew Tilghman.

By mid-1775, he was an officer of the Council of Safety for the state, overseeing, among other things, the acquisition of arms and ammunition for the county militias. At one point, he was personally in charge of ordering five thousand cartridge boxes to hold the paper tubes of black powder and ball used in the muzzle-loading weapons.

For his good work, Alexander found himself appointed a Maryland delegate to the Continental Congress. He arrived in Philadelphia in January of 1776 and took a seat beside Maryland rebels Samuel Chase and William Paca. Soon placed on several different committees, Alexander settled into the business at hand. Of course, to Alexander the business at hand was establishing the rights of the colonists. It was poetic justice perhaps that he served on a committee with John Dickinson and James Wilson, both of whom strongly defended the colonies against arbitrary rule yet disavowed the idea that Congress was carrying on the war "for the purpose of establishing an independent Empire.... We disavow the Intention."[12] Others in Congress, though, *were* avowing the intention and the countdown to independence had already started.

Alexander's patriotic fervor began to wane. He was now digging into his own pocket to pay for the shipment of cartridge paper he had ordered for the Maryland troops. The Continental Congressman wrote to the Council of Safety complaining of the greed of merchants. Annoyed by the mercenary interests of these suppliers, he declared, "Patriotism sinks before private Interest."[13] This loss of idealism was spreading: George Washington would express similar dissatisfaction with soldiers under his command. Despite his misgivings, though, Alexander continued to procure gunpowder and other supplies for Maryland.

By May, however, when it became abundantly clear that independence, not reconciliation, was the goal of the Congress, Alexander withdrew from the Maryland delegation, but not from public life: He would soon hold an important political position—for the British.

Tories and Rebels

The rebellious colonists in Maryland scored their first big victory in Maryland on the Eastern Shore. This was more than a little ironic considering the deep pockets of loyalism that existed in the region.

On May 23, 1774, a ship named the *Geddes* docked at New Town (later renamed Chestertown and so-called herein) with a shipment of English tea in its hold. The captain of the *Geddes* had picked a bad time to arrive. Just two months had elapsed since the Boston Tea Party. Fueled by the recent news from Boston, some angry citizens boarded the ship and tossed the tea into the Chester River.[14] In local history, it was dubbed the "Chestertown Tea Party." The event brought mixed reviews. Some were only too happy to bring things to a head. Others, more sympathetic to England, feared what was coming.

By the fall of 1775, the divisions on the Eastern Shore were becoming very apparent. Neighbors were now enemies and everyone spied on everyone else's activities. British ships moved in and out of the lower part of the Bay, intimidating rebels and trading with the local loyalists. To counter the problem, loyalists were discouraged in their activities and threatened with violence.

The Eastern Shore branch of the Council of Safety met regularly at Chestertown, which was the largest Maryland town east of the Chesapeake. Meetings were punctuated by local citizens informing on their tory neighbors. There was no end of things to inform on.

In November, patriotic informants told the council that Levin Townsend of Worcester County ventured out to one of the British ships in the Bay and brought back a quantity of ammunition. Shortly after, it was reported that a number of loyalists were invited to his father's house for a share of the supplies. Townsend allegedly told his visitors that if they signed a piece of paper, he would be able to get assistance from the nearby warship.[15]

Just as dangerous to the Eastern Shore whigs was the report concerning Isaac Atkinson of Somerset County. In September of 1775, the militia company of Captain George Day Scott was mustering at the lower ferry of the Wicomico River to enlist recruits and choose officers. The drummer was ordered to beat "to arms" and the ragtag fishermen and farmers began to fall into ranks alongside the road. It was quickly observed that at least half the men had formed up on the opposite side of the road from the others and had placed red cockades (rosettes of ribbons) in their hats rather than the usual black.

Seeing that they were under the leadership of a sergeant named Isaac Atkinson, Captain Scott confronted him. It was soon revealed that Atkinson had told his men to bring sharp flints for their muskets to the muster, a gesture which spoke loud and clear of an intention to do more than simply parade their arms. He produced his powder horn and declared they intended to fire their guns as a salute to the breaking up of the company.

Scott asked Atkinson if he was raising his company in opposition to the resolves of the Congress and provincial convention. In a voice described by a witness as "cool and calm," Atkinson said he was and wanted to bet a doubloon that he could recruit hundreds of men to join him in opposition to the state council. A man in his company chimed in, "Yes, a thousand men, ten to one, if they are wanted; for he is the only man that has opened our eyes; and he is the man that ought to be upheld."

Predictably, Atkinson was soon brought before the Committee of Observation for Somerset County where various neighbors made depositions against him. In one statement, Atkinson had been heard to say that "the people of Boston wanted a King of their own in America." Atkinson denied the charges. Outside the courthouse, Atkinson's cohorts gathered with short clubs looking for trouble. When Atkinson appeared, a crowd of fifty supporters gathered around him. Boldly, he told them, "A day must be appointed and they must fight it out." But for Atkinson, the fight was over: he was soon detained.[16] Insurrection, though, was to be a continual threat on the Eastern Shore for years to come.

The colonists, whigs and tories alike, would have been quite surprised to discover the conflict wasn't popular in England. A number of English citizens were opposed to taking up arms against Americans since so many of them had relatives in the colonies. At about the same time, loyalist Samuel Curwen, an exiled New England loyalist living in London, related in his journal what happened to his landlady on a recent coach trip:

> The Islington stage coach was stopped [and] a young fellow in a military Habit soon appearing was admitted into the coach; he seemed somewhat apprehensive, frightened, on which she asked him the reason, but before he could answer, 3 ordinary fellows came out cursing and calling him foul names and swore if they could have catched him they would have given him a hearty drubbing. . . . he then told the company it was usage he was lately accustomed to, saying further that he was going to America and had been on the recruiting service but was unsuccessful; as that service was disgustful to the common people; and rendered the officers hateful, and obnoxious to them and liable to daily affronts and abuses. The fellows finding him out of their reach threw mud and sticks at the Coach to manifest their resentment at him and his business.[17]

Back in Maryland, there were hundreds of men very willing to fight the rebels. Without a central leader, however, the loyalist movement on the Eastern Shore had been sporadic and ineffective. But that was about to change.

James Chalmers and Plain Truth

Shall we harbour such villains in our bosom?
—The Reverend James Josias Wilmer
(speaking of James Chalmers)

In January and February of 1776, Philadelphia, not New England, was the epicenter of the conflict with Great Britain. Despite bloodshed at Lexington and Concord and terrible losses at Bunker Hill, tories and a few moderate whigs hoped in vain for a last-minute reconciliation with the mother country.

The motives for wanting such a miracle were quite naturally divided along party lines. The tories sought an end to the conflict before armed resistance spread throughout the colonies; some whigs, on the other hand, felt they had flexed their muscles enough to show they were serious about not submitting to England's arbitrary rule of the colonies. The consequences of resistance, however, were to go beyond what most colonists and Britons expected. Rebellion was about to become revolution, largely because of a simple pamphlet. On Wednesday, January 10, 1776, the words of a virtually unknown English dissident would change the world forever.

Thomas Paine's *Common Sense* hit like a lightning bolt in the colonies. Its message was simple: Britain had no right to govern America, the monarchical system itself was basically corrupt, and Americans would be much better off on their own. His arguments certainly struck a chord. The French and Indian War of the 1750s had shown the colonists just how far they had drifted from their English counterparts in nearly every aspect of politics and culture. England saw colonists as crude and uneducated, while the English were seen as drunk with power and subservient to a monarchy that had no meaning to the average colonist, who pretty much lived by his own rules.

Not everyone, though, read Paine's work and nodded with approval. Hard-core loyalists were realizing that they had been blindsided by a powerful piece of propaganda. Anxious to put out the fires that *Common Sense* was igniting, they attempted to strike back. One of the very first to do so was a gentleman of means from the colony of Maryland—a planter named James Chalmers.

"This Worthy Character"

Chalmers's life is something of a mystery. His early years, pieced together from what he told the British government after the war, revealed the story of a man of ambition. Born in Scotland in 1727, he went to the British West Indies when he was thirteen years old. His profession there for the next twenty years is unclear, although his obituary seems to hint at some kind of military service during this time. One thing we know for sure is that, by the time he left, he had made a lot of money. In the West Indies, the eighteenth-century roads to wealth were the sugar, rum, and slave trade. Like most white men of the time, the concept of owning human beings didn't seem to trouble him very much.

In 1760, Chalmers arrived in Maryland with several black slaves and a hefty ten thousand British pounds in his purse. This substantial sum made it easy for him to become a farmer and landowner of great standing on the Eastern Shore. Before long, he owned several thousand acres around Chestertown in Kent County. His wealth gave him a certain amount of influence, which he spent the rest of his life trying to exert.

He certainly seemed to be making friends in the right places. In 1769, Englishman William Eddis took a trip with Maryland Governor Robert Eden and a party of gentlemen to the Eastern Shore where they were lavishly entertained for a day by Chalmers. In his notes for October 19, Eddis described the Maryland loyalist as "our friendly host" and observed a prophetic aspect of his personality:

> This gentleman resides on an island in the Chesapeake, about seven miles in length and of different breadth; the whole of which, being his entire property, is well cultivated . . . the worthy proprietor lives in a manner independent of mankind, the *monarch* [emphasis added] of his little fertile territory.

Some time in 1775, he appears to have been offered a regiment in the rebel service. This isn't as peculiar as it sounds. The conflict still centered around resistance, not revolution. Chalmers, however, turned down the offer and requests to attend rebel committees. By his own admission, he armed his family in Chestertown and prepared to "repel force by force."[1]

"Well-bred and well-informed," despite "the strong peculiarities of his temper, manner, address, and diction," Chalmers is further described as "a sound disciplinarian, resolute, strict, and humane."[2] When war came, this well-read but irritable Scotsman had had enough. Surrounding himself with wealthy Eastern Shore loyalists, Chalmers was to become lieutenant colonel of the First Battalion of Maryland Loyalists a little over a year after writing *Plain Truth*, his famous rebuttal to *Common Sense*.

PLAIN TRUTH

Nestled in a building on South Third Street beside Saint Paul's Episcopal Church was Philadelphia's most popular bookstore. Robert Bell's shop carried books on the arts, sciences, languages, history, biography, divinity, law, voyages, travels, poetry, plays, novels, and virtually anything else the well-read eighteenth-century gentleman might care to peruse.[3] Bell also published pamphlets, and Chalmers was only too anxious to see his thoughts appear in the best bookshop in town. Chalmers must have enjoyed the ironic fact that it was Robert Bell who had published the first edition of *Common Sense*.

On Saturday, March 16, 1776, an advertisement first appeared in the *Pennsylvania Ledger*, a local newspaper which favored loyalist views. For three shillings, interested citizens could purchase *Plain Truth; addressed to the Inhabitants of America*. Written under the name "Candidus," James Chalmers launched an all-out assault on Paine's work. In the space of seventy pages, he resorted to everything he could think of to tear down *Common Sense*. For those who just couldn't get enough of the Maryland loyalist's writings, *Additions to Plain Truth* appeared on April 10 for only one shilling.

Unfortunately for Chalmers, he had done precisely the wrong thing. While Paine had written in the plainest language possible in order to reach the common man with his argument, Chalmers took the high road with a strong emphasis on literary references and history through the ages. A semiliterate blacksmith who could muddle his way through *Common Sense* must have looked at *Plain Truth* and shrugged his shoulders. Many educated and learned men were already loyalists; it was the "great unwashed" who needed convincing that England was still their sovereign.

Chalmers began his work, in supreme flowery form, with a dedication to John Dickinson, the famous representative of Pennsylvania at the Continental Congress. He acknowledged, "I have not the Honor to be Known to You," to which the reader can easily fill in what must have been his next thought, ". . . but I would certainly like to be known to you." These were the words of a man who never feared the taste of boot polish.

Step then forth; exert those Talents with which HEAVEN has endowed you; and cause the Parent, and her Children to embrace, and be foes no more. Arduous as this extraordinary talk may seem, perhaps your Virtue and Talents, may yet effect it. Your Endeavors to stop the Effusion of Blood, of Torrents of Blood, is worthy of your acknowledged Humanity—Even the honest attempt upon recollection, will afford you ineffable satisfaction.[4]

> *Juſt printed, publiſhed, and now ſelling by*
> ROBERT BELL, in Third ſtreet, Philadelphia, *Price Three Shillings, with large allowance to thoſe who buy per the hundred or dozen.*
> PLAIN TRUTH; addreſſed to the INHABITANTS of AMERICA, containing Remarks on a late Pamphlet intituled COMMON SENSE. Wherein are ſhewn, that the Scheme of INDEPENDENCE is Ruinous, Deluſive, and impracticable: That were the Author's Aſſeverations, reſpecting the Power of AMERICA, as Real as Nugatory, Reconciliation, on liberal Principles with GREAT-BRITAIN would be exalted Policy: And that, circumſtanced as we are, permanent Liberty, and true Happineſs can only be obtained by Reconciliation with that Kingdom. Written by CANDIDUS.
> Will ye turn from Flattery and attend to this ſide?
> *There* Truth, *unlicenc'd, walks; and dares accoſt Even Kings themſelves, the Monarchs of the Free!*
> Thompſon *on the Liberties of* Britain.
> N. B. To this Pamphlet is ſubjoined a Defence of the Liberty of the Preſs, by the ſagacious and partriotic JUNIUS, Author of the celebrated FREE Letters to his preſent Majeſty, and his Miniſters.

Advertisement for *Plain Truth, Pennsylvania Ledger,* March 16, 1776. Its appearance came shortly after the British evacuation of Boston.

PLAIN TRUTH;

ADDRESSED TO THE

INHABITANTS

OF

AMERICA,

Containing, Remarks

ON A LATE PAMPHLET,

entitled

COMMON SENSE.

Wherein are fhewn, that the Scheme of INDEPENDENCE is Ruinous, Delufive, and Inpracticable : That were the Author's Affeverations, Refpecting the Power of AMERICA, as Real as Nugatory ; Reconciliation on liberal Principles with GREAT BRITAIN, would be exalted Policy : And that circumftanced as we are, Permanant Liberty, and True Happinefs, can only be obtained by Reconciliation with that Kingdom.

WRITTEN BY CANDIDUS.

Audi et alterem partem. HORACE.

Will ye turn from flattery, and attend to this Side?

There TRUTH, unlicenc'd, walks; and dares accoft
Even Kings themfelves, the Monarchs of the Free!
THOMSON on the Liberties of BRITAIN.

PHILADELPHIA:
Printed, and Sold, by R. BELL, in Third-Street.

MDCCLXXVI.

The title page of Chalmers's pamphlet, March 1776. The Maryland loyalist's remarks were already too late. Philadelphia was on its inevitable way toward independence.

As complimentary as this may be, Chalmers had more in mind than mere flattery. A man like John Dickinson was exactly what a man like Chalmers wanted to be: a powerful and influential colonist, respectful of England, mindful of colonists' concerns, and, most importantly, a man who could influence millions with his writings.

In a series of letters to the *Pennsylvania Chronicle* in 1767 and 1768, Dickinson wrote in no uncertain terms that Parliament lacked the authority to tax the colonies simply because it needed revenue. Entitled *Letters from a Farmer in Pennsylvania to Inhabitants of the British Colonies*, Dickinson's words were read throughout the colonies as well as in England, causing quite a stir. In subsequent years, Dickinson would rise to the forefront of reform. To loyalists, moderate men like Dickinson seemed the last hope to end the fighting. Unfortunately for Chalmers, Dickinson later refused to endorse his pamphlet.

Chalmers, by his admission, chose to write *Plain Truth* after waiting week upon week for someone to respond with anger to *Common Sense*. None did. New York's *Constitutional Gazette* called Paine's work "a wonderful production," while others were equally complimentary. Sensing great opposition, the Kent County planter boldly took the initiative.

No time was wasted as he called Paine a "political quack" and took offense at the man's attack upon the English constitution. "With all its imperfections [the English constitution] is, and ever will be, the pride and envy of mankind."[5] This was a safe argument in March 1776. The Declaration of Independence, which so elegantly expressed the dissatisfied American point of view, did not yet exist. The rebellion itself was being propelled mostly by a few loud orators from New England. No one, of course, had suggested how colonists could come up with something better than England's system of laws. Loyalists like Chalmers were banking on the hope that they never would.

A ripe target in *Plain Truth* was Paine's love of democracy. Few now realize that the word "democracy" didn't have a particularly appealing ring to it in the eighteenth century. Even radical John Adams, a man who was pushing hard for independence, was nervous about Paine's brand of unregulated democracy. It "was so democratical, without any restraint or even an attempt at any equilibrium or counterpoise, that it must produce confusion and every evil work," he once wrote.[6] Later in life, he declared, "What a poor ignorant, Malicious, short-sighted, Crapulous Mass, is Tom Pains Common Sense."[7] For one fleeting moment, Chalmers and John Adams actually agreed on something.

Adams may have been a radical but he was no one's fool. He knew any new government would have to be run by politicians and not by mob leaders. To many whigs and tories alike, democracy for its own sake didn't seem like an especially good idea. Historically, democracies had come and gone, a fact that Chalmers doesn't hesitate to point out.

> The demogogues to seduce the people into their criminal designs ever hold up democracy to them. . . . If we examine the republics of Greece and Rome, we ever find them in a state of war domestic or foreign. . . . Apian's history of the civil wars of Rome, contains the most frightful picture of massacres . . . that ever were presented to the world.[8]

Mistrustful of France and her intentions, Chalmers was compelled to remind his readers of the great debt owed England by the colonies. Citing William Penn and the Pennsylvania Quakers as settlers who brought "toleration, industry, and permanent credit" to the colonies, Chalmers says England took proper notice.

> The people of England, encouraged by the extension of their laws and commerce to those colonies, powerfully assisted our merchants and planters, insomuch, that our settlements increased rapidly. . . . It may be affirmed, that from this period, until the present unhappy hour; no part of human kind, ever experienced more perfect felicity. Voltaire indeed says, that if ever the Golden Age existed, it was in Pennsylvania.[9]

Chalmers was on firm ground with this argument and he knew it. By the time of the Revolution, the American colonies were about the best place in the world to live. Opportunity was everywhere, land on the frontier was for the taking (or stealing, as the case may be), and taxes were almost nonexistent in comparison to what the inhabitants of England were forced to pay. Best of all, the heavy-handed authority of King George and Parliament was diffused by several thousand miles of ocean.

At this point, he mentioned the French and Indian War only in passing by saying, "In the hour of our distress, we called aloud on Great Britain for assistance, nor was she deaf to our cries." This strong sense of obligation to England for defeating France is curiously understated by Chalmers. It may have been a matter he considered so obvious that it didn't require special attention.

To dispel Paine's hints that England and the rest of Europe were becoming dependent on American wheat, Chalmers sardonically asserted, "I believe the Europeans did eat before our merchants exported our grain." Citing a drought in Poland and the Ukraine as the cause of the sudden increase in exports, Chalmers denied that "this momentary commerce" had much effect on the colonies. As proof, he said, "the most fertile and delectable wheat country in America, bounded by Chesapeak-bay," was terribly underdeveloped. Lack of manpower, industry, and wealth were the prime culprits. He implied that those industrious few who cultivated the land in this area had done quite well for themselves.

It isn't very difficult to gather from his description that the cultivated Maryland land he talked about was, of course, his own in Kent County that he later called "the best Lands in America."[10] No one would ever accuse James Chalmers of modesty.

The British West Indies inevitably arose in any discussion of colonial trade. Chalmers wanted very much to convey his own experience concerning this vital link of trade to the British Empire: "We are unacquainted with the West India Islands, if we believe that they solely depend on us for provisions and lumber. . . . I know it will be re-echoed that the West India Islands cannot do without America. The contrary is nevertheless true."[11]

This economic argument was one of Chalmers's worst miscalculations. Quite simply, he should have known better. For someone who had spent so much time in the British West Indies, he seemed to have absolutely no clue of the power the colonies had over the Caribbean islands in terms of trade. When war came, the West Indies were crippled by Britain's effective blockade of the tropical ports. The loss of trade may have denied money to the colonies, but it also denied timber and other needed supplies to the sugar islands.[12] A distinct preoccupation with the West Indies would make itself known over and over again until the end of Chalmers's life.

After a few distractions, he moved on to the heart of all loyalist arguments: the colonists couldn't possibly win a war against Great Britain. At every level, England outgunned and outmanned the colonies. On paper, the weakness of the colonies was almost comical. A nonexistent navy, badly disciplined recruits, and a great scarcity of heavy industry to produce arms and ammunition combined to create the picture of a colony of wishful thinkers who didn't stand a chance once England roused what Shakespeare called "its sleeping sword."

Then, Chalmers did a curious thing: he spoke of his pride in the army that the colonies had raised. "I am under no doubt, however, that we shall become as famed for martial courage, as any nation ever the sun beheld," he stated enthusiastically.[13] These are, of course, the same troops who wiped out rank after rank of redcoats on Breed's Hill in Boston just eight months before. It turned out to be a backhanded compliment because Chalmers felt that a simple desire for liberty wasn't enough to keep the colonists from losing a war with England. Alone, they didn't stand a chance. To win, they would have to have a great European power such as France or Spain on their side.

Here, Chalmers made an important and often overlooked observation: he found it illogical for any foreign power to side with the colonists against England, and with good reason.

> Can we be so deluded, to expect aid from those princes [France and Spain], which inspiring their subjects with a relish for liberty, might eventually shake their arbitrary thrones. . . . Can we believe that those princes will offer an example so dangerous to their subjects and colonies . . . ?[14]

One can't help but think that if King Louis XVI of France had read this passage of Chalmers's pamphlet, he might have saved his own life. On this point, Chalmers couldn't have unknowingly foretold the future with any greater exactness. France *was* deluded enough to aid the colonists, the French people *were* inspired with a relish for liberty, and they *did* shake the arbitrary throne by relieving the king of his head in the French Revolution.

For his part, Chalmers couldn't imagine that a country like France would be foolish enough to join the fight. But against the expectations of loyalists and rebels alike, France did leap into the war effort with money, arms, and troops, making victory for England much less likely. That situation, however, was still years away.

In *Plain Truth*, Chalmers was blunt about the resolve of England to put down the rebellion.

> Can a reasonable being for a moment believe that Great Britain, whose political existence depends on our constitutional obedience, who but yesterday made such prodigious efforts to save us from France, will not exert herself as powerfully to preserve us from our frantic schemes of independency. Can we a moment doubt, that the Sovereign of Great Britain and his ministers, whose glory as well as personal safety depends on our obedience, will not exert every nerve of the British power, to save themselves and us from ruin[?][15]

This, of course, was a great sticking point for those colonists who didn't know which side to join. The revolutionaries talked of their own resolve, but what of England's? They couldn't afford to lose the colonies, could they?

Chalmers himself made a surprising admission when he stated, "I see no reason to doubt that Great Britain may not long retain us in constitutional obedience." Despite her powerful position in the world, Chalmers confessed that "time, the destroyer of human affairs, may indeed end her political life by a gentle decay." It was a subtle, but definite admission that aligned him far closer to Thomas Paine then he would have liked to admit. For all his posturing, Chalmers was not an Englishman; he was a displaced Scotsman and enterprising colonist. It would take a bitter war, the loss of his lands, and the ruination of his reputation in Maryland to turn Chalmers into an unflinching Englishman in his later years.

He ended *Plain Truth* with a stark, Orwellian statement. The final line, in capital letters, reads: INDEPENDENCE AND SLAVERY ARE SYNONYMOUS TERMS.

It was an odd pamphlet indeed. Filled with all of the politically incorrect stances of the 1700s, *Plain Truth* hints at Chalmers's indifference to the slave trade and his openly anti-Semitic views. One oddity was his deferential comments toward Native Americans. Few care to notice that the Declaration of Independence refers to Native Americans as "merciless Indian Savages." In a few passing comments, Chalmers, in contrast to most whites of the time, treated the original inhabitants of America with respect. A hint of wisdom could not, however, make up for a multitude of sins. Seldom concise, often wandering off on tangents, *Plain Truth* reflected one man's gut reactions.

Other loyalists would write on the same subjects with greater eloquence, but all would come after *Plain Truth*.

And Chalmers had still more to say.

"AT LIBERTY TO SPEAK"

Intended to solidify the arguments of the hastily written original pamphlet, *Additions to Plain Truth* shows Chalmers a month later and just as

Philadelphia, April 10, 1776.
Juſt Printed, Publiſhed, and now ſelling, By
ROBERT BELL,
Printer in Third-ſtreet, Price only *One Shilling, with large allowance to thoſe who buy per dozen:*

Additions to Plain Truth:

Addreſſed to the INHABITANTS of AMERICA Containing further Remarks on a late Pamphlet, entitled

COMMON SENSE:

Wherein are clearly and fully ſhewn, that American Independence, is as illuſory, ruinous, and impracticable, as a liberal reconciliation with Great Britain, is ſafe, honourable, and expedient.

WRITTEN by the AUTHOR of PLAIN TRUTH.

The enjoyment of Liberty, and even its ſupport and preſervation conſiſts, in every man's being allowed to ſpeak his thoughts and lay open his ſentiments.

Quotations of the American CONGRESS, in their Addreſs to the Inhabitants of Quebec, from that Friend to Mankind, *Monteſquieu.*

N. B. To this Pamphlet is annexed, for the information of all *Americans,* who wiſh to know and to enjoy the very *Laws* and *Privileges* which themſelves have decreed. A *Defence* of the *Liberty* of the *Preſs,* by the Honorable the CONTINENTAL CONGRESS

Memorandum. If to preſerve any part of the works of valuable writers, hath always been looked upon as doing good ſervice to the *Public;* The EDITOR hereof may hope, that his preſent endeavours will prove acceptable, at leaſt, to all the *Lovers* of *Freedom,* who are ſo conſiſtent as to acknowledge the *Preſs* ought to be *free* for *others* as well as *themſelves.*

Fans of *Plain Truth* did not have to wait long for the sequel: advertisement for *Additions to Plain Truth, Pennsylvania Ledger,* May 4, 1776.

angry. He quickly reminded his readers of the "Antichristian tenets" which Paine expressed in *Common Sense*. (Ironically, Chalmers's fellow citizens reached the same conclusion and declared Paine an atheist. Unfortunately, that wouldn't happen for another twenty-five years.)

After restating old arguments, he reminded his readers of the terrible price of war: "Should this war prove unsuccessful on the part of Great Britain, we cannot imagine that it will terminate, e'er many bloody fields are lost and won; I say, it probably will not end in less than 10 years."[16]

Having presented his thoughts on how long a war would last, he asked his readers if they were ready to drench the colonies in blood. Even more to the point, he wanted to know if the colonists were prepared to die for the "restless ambition" of Thomas Paine. Chalmers viewed such a war as an effort totally in vain. He believed his fellow citizens were impelled "by their turbulent ambition to anticipate an event which the fullness of time would probably produce without bloodshed."[17]

This one statement does much to dispel the notion that loyalists were simply "yes-men" to the king and Parliament. The loyalists' philosophy and their intentions were not those of England, to which they professed allegiance. In truth, their concerns, in many respects, weren't really much different from those of their revolutionary counterparts. Both sides wanted the colonies to be prosperous. Both sides saw Great Britain making sudden and heavy-handed attempts to display its authority over its offspring.

Despite his earlier glowing reviews of English authority, even Chalmers came to admit that the colonies were a separate entity. Whig and tory could see that England was the problem; they just couldn't agree on the solution. Like most loyalists, Chalmers saw reconciliation as the answer, the only answer.

> In short, let us remember, that by our connection with Great Britain, we have been the happiest people on earth, and by

a just agreement with her we may long continue so. Let us dispassionately consider, that in a connection with Great Britain, we may possess all the ROSES of independence, without being cursed with its innumerable THORNS.[18]

Once again, he was certain that for all the complaining about how England operated, the colonies could not and would not come up with a better system of government. Recalling his earlier pamphlet, Chalmers insisted a democratic government would eventually give way to a "military system" imposed on the colonies. While he admitted this wouldn't happen under General Washington (whom he called a "virtuous citizen"), he was certain that it was only a matter of time. Perhaps, he mused, it would be instigated by some junior officer whose talents for tyranny were, as yet, unknown.[19]

Although *Plain Truth* apparently sold without incident in Philadelphia, Chalmers told his readers that whig officials in New York had a great aversion to the pamphlet and, consequently, a number of copies sent to New York City were seized. He was struck by the sheer irony of the situation. The pamphlet was selling literally under the "immediate eye" of the Continental Congress without trouble, yet was confiscated elsewhere. Here he encountered the dark underbelly of the American Revolution.

The rebels' actions showed a double standard that was offensive to Chalmers: "If such doings are the first fruits of REPUBLICAN LIBERTY? Grant me Heaven, our former mild and limited Government, where the prerogative is ascertained by law, and where every man is at liberty to speak and print his sentiments."[20]

The question was quite justified. More than most wars in history, this was a struggle of competing ideologies. For the rebels to win their war for independence and the liberty that they deemed so vital, it was necessary to suppress any and all dissent in the colonies. Their message was essentially, "We're fighting against tyranny and you'll agree completely with us, or else!" It was a bitter pill for loyalists to swallow.

Chalmers concluded *Additions to Plain Truth* with a final appeal to reason:

> Let us remember that reconciliation on generous principles with Great Britain, is our true and only road to permanent happiness. Above all, let us seriously consider, that this when the commissioners arrive to treat with the Congress is the juncture, this the moment, when we may receive everything we can reasonably desire.
>
> I conclude these remarks, by observing, that if they are founded in truth, they will instruct you to keep a good look out, that ye may not be surprized into AMERICAN INDEPENDENCY; without a thorough examination of it, and its consequences.

Plain Truth would prove a failed document, doomed from the very start. Its first appearance on Robert Bell's bookshelf occurred within days of one of the rebels' greatest accomplishments. In Boston, the British had pulled out their occupying forces when they woke up one morning to find a battery of rebel artillery, "borrowed" from Fort Ticonderoga, bearing down on them. Winning a war against the redcoats suddenly seemed possible. Chalmers's pleas for making peace with England couldn't have been more ill-timed.

He may not have turned the tide, but *Plain Truth* was widely read. Just a few weeks after its appearance, a writer calling himself "Cato" spoke favorably of Chalmers in a letter to the people of Pennsylvania published in the *Pennsylvania Ledger*. Mentioning the recent pamphlet, the writer recommended it "as containing many judicious remarks upon the mischievous tenets and palpable absurdities held forth in the pamphlet so falsely called *Common Sense*."[21]

An edition appeared in England as well. In his journal on Monday, June 10, exiled New England loyalist Samuel Curwen noted that he spent all day reading *Common Sense* and *Plain Truth* at his London home.[22] Unfortunately, he never gave his opinion of either work.

Throughout the years, though, others have been more than happy to pass judgment on *Plain Truth*. Historians have often been very unforgiving, calling it everything from "ponderous" and "forgettable" to "atrociously written." Yes, Chalmers does meander quite a bit in his writing, at times reluctant to come to the point. It should be remembered, though, that this isn't very unusual in eighteenth-century writing. Even John Adams and Thomas Jefferson, possibly the two most articulate men in the colonies, would put many modern readers to sleep with their lengthy discourses on philosophy and religion.

In later years, *Plain Truth* would fade into utter obscurity. In 1776, however, Chalmers was an influential loyalist. A little more than a year later, he would sit down with General Sir William Howe, commander of British forces in America. Howe was impressed with his abilities and commissioned him to raise a regiment of Maryland loyalists.

Chalmers must have thought his star was on the rise. What followed, however, were six years of disappointment.

3

Conflict

Then, brave boys, we both France and the Congress defy,
And we'll fight for Great Britain and George till we die.

—A loyalist song

Insurrection, High Treason, and Other Diversions

If it wasn't a war before, it was now. With the Declaration of Independence, the united colonies were suddenly the United States. Suppression of tories was now more important than ever.

In Maryland, oaths of fidelity were demanded. The state council, by its own admission, had designed the oath to act essentially as a pardon.[1] They weren't naive enough to believe these people were now committed patriots. The oaths more or less meant, "We won't put you in jail but you better keep your mouth shut or you'll be sorry."

After a crushing defeat in New York, the surprise American victories at Trenton and Princeton gave the rebellion new life, and a new desire to stamp out tory activity arose. In the afterglow of Trenton, James Chalmers was attacked by an angry mob in Chestertown and, as he claimed, "his life was imminently endangered."[2] The attack had been abetted by "a Colonel Perkins," who, there's good reason to believe, may have been Isaac Perkins, a Kent County mill owner. As wheat was his main crop, Chalmers would likely have had business dealings with Perkins before the war. (Chalmers seems to have gotten his revenge five years later when Perkins's mill was burned down by local tories, destroying shipments of flour meant for the Continental Army.[3])

Loyalist discontent was rising on the Eastern Shore, threatening any stability the patriots had. Samuel Chase, Maryland delegate to the Continental Congress, acquired intelligence of the situation and knew action was necessary. He wrote the council on February 6, 1777:

> The Tories in Sussex [Delaware], Somerset and Worcester Counties, have been assembling for some days. They have 250 men collected at Parker's Mill, about nine miles from Salisbury, and 'tis reported they have three field pieces, which they received from the *Roebuck* [a 44-gun British man-of-war], with some men, with intention to seise the Magazine and destroy the property of the Whiggs.... There are three men of war in the bay, one at the Tangiers, one at Smith's point, and one in the middle.... I must again repeat the necessity of a Representation.[4]

Brigadier General William Smallwood, the commander of Maryland's army, arrived on the Eastern Shore with soldiers to put down the insurrection. He had little tolerance for dissent. From Snow Hill, he wrote:

> What have you to expect from those who have cut down the Liberty Poles, and in direct opposition thereto, have erected the Kings Standard, & in an avowed manner drank his Health and Success & destruction to Congress and Conventions.... What can be expected from the Inhabitants of a Place which becomes the Reception of Deserters, escaping Prisoners, and most of the Disaffected who have been expelled [from] the neighbouring States.... [They] make Religion a Cloak for their nefarious Designs.[5]

Whatever nefarious designs the loyalists had, a strong show of force by Smallwood and his combined army of nearly three thousand soldiers put an end to the insurrection. Some loyalists fled, some simply went underground and kept quiet. The revolutionaries had little time to celebrate their victory, however, for a new threat was arising that was far bigger than local tory unrest.

Rebel spies were hard at work watching the British and they knew something was up. As early as April 2, 1777, John Hancock, president of the Continental Congress, wrote to Maryland Governor Thomas Johnson, saying: "Our Enemies are meditating an Invasion of the State of Maryland. In this Situation of Affairs, I am earnestly to request you will take such measures as will have a Tendency to defeat their designs should any Attempts be made in consequence of this intelligence."[6]

Howe wanted the rebel capital of Philadelphia. It was traditional military wisdom to capture the enemy's base of government. For months, the British kept the rebels guessing as to how they would launch an invasion force from New York to Philadelphia. Would they go by ship via the Delaware River or the Chesapeake Bay? Would they attempt to cross New Jersey and march into the capital?

In June, James Chalmers was in New York City where he advised Howe through his aide-de-camp that in April he had been in New Jersey and observed the weakness of Washington's army, then lying at the Raritan River. Chalmers perceived they could be overcome with relative ease, thereby clearing a path to Philadelphia in four days' time as opposed to a lengthy trip up the Bay.[7] Chalmers was ignored, but it wouldn't be the last time he offered advice to his superiors.

A Visit from the Men in Red

In August 1777, an enormous fleet of British ships sailed up the Chesapeake. Among other things, they indulged in the time-honored tradition of every visitor to Maryland—they had a crab feast. Captain John Montresor, chief engineer for the British Army in America, observed in his journal: "August 20th: At 6 P.M., the Fleet came to anchor off of

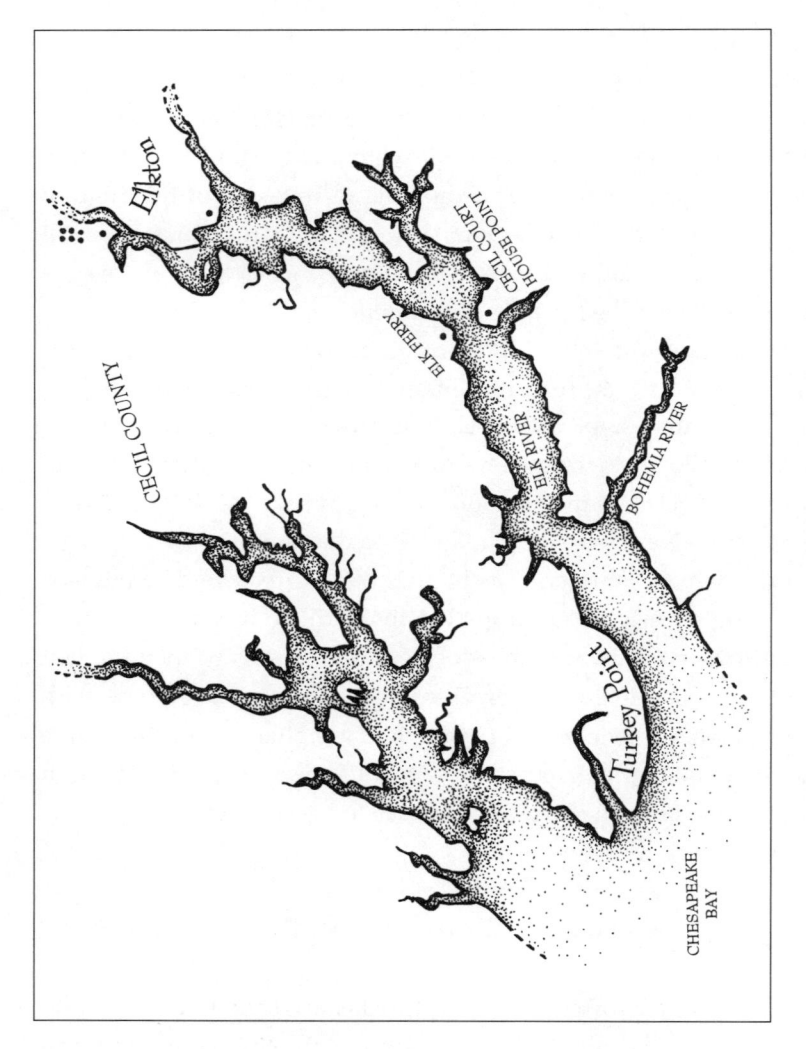

"The British Landing at Head Elk": landing at Elk Ferry, the British made their way north to present-day Elkton (based on a contemporary map).

Poplar Island. . . . It's remarkable in this Bay the multitude of crabs that swim nearly to the surface of the water. The Fleet caught thousands."[8]

It was an enormous fleet, twenty-five warships transporting some eighteen thousand men. Their objective was the Head of Elk, site of present-day Elkton, Maryland. From there, they would march overland into the rebel capital of Philadelphia.

The following morning at seven, the fleet sailed past Annapolis without exchanging fire with the defenses on shore. Governor Johnson had ordered the women, children, servants, and slaves to quit the town just the day before.[9] The men left to defend the city were more interested in removing arms and ammunition than fighting such an overwhelming show of force. The British wouldn't see a fight here. Nature, however, wasn't so cooperative. Lightning strikes killed several men and horses.

The next day, Friday, August 22, Montresor observed, "Several of our people in the Fleet [are] on shore, some at Newtown [Chestertown] on Chester River." Although not mentioned by name, one of those in Newtown was undoubtedly James Chalmers. As the Maryland loyalist would later admit, he took his leave from the British fleet and quietly landed near Chestertown, hiding himself in the home of his pastor, The Reverend John Paterson. He gathered intelligence from Paterson and a Chestertown loyalist named William Slubey. Chalmers later rejoined the British ships without detection. It would be some time before the state council learned all the details of this spy mission. It didn't, however, take them long to figure out that Paterson was involved and the reverend soon found himself an unwilling guest of the state. William Paca wrote Governor Thomas Johnson:

> I herewith send you a most incorrigible fellow, the Rev. John Paterson; he has been endeavouring to throw every obstacle in the way to calling forth our militia, and has violated the Execution of our Laws; he is the most provoking exasperating mortal that ever existed. We have great reasons to suspect him of being concerned with one Chambers [Chal-

mers] of this county who is now with the Enemy conducting them on their ravaging and plundering Parties.[10]

The Reverend James Josias Wilmer, also from Chestertown, mentioned the other accomplice of Chalmers in his own letter to the governor, saying that William Slubey "was privy to the infamous James Chalmers being in Chestertown who was sent by the British commander to collect a true state of the Eastern Shore."[11]

Slubey and other loyalists were said to have spoken with Chalmers about the possibility of making William Paca a prisoner of the British. In addition, Wilmer was convinced that Chalmers's friends "kept runners to and from N[ew] York under the sanction of a petticoat."

An emotional Reverend Wilmer proclaimed, "Shall we at this time, when such proofs can be well attested, harbour such villains in our bosom?"[12] The state council apparently didn't think so. Chalmers was believed guilty of treason, as were those who had aided or sheltered him during his visit.[13]

At some point before rejoining the British fleet, Chalmers must have made arrangements with local tories to procure horses and cattle for the British when they landed at the Head of Elk. Another Eastern Shore resident, Daniel Heath, was also in the cattle business with the British. He, however, was a bit more underhanded than most. A few months after the invasion, wealthy Kent County landowner James Frisby, newly arrived in Philadelphia to join the British, carelessly told a rebel spy of loyalist dealings in Maryland. It came out that Heath had convinced his neighbors to put their cattle into his pastures for "protection and that Heath had sold them to the [British] Fleet and had got for them a very large bagg of Gold."[14]

Two days later, on August 24, the fleet had made it as far north as Turkey Point at the mouth of the Elk River. Major John André, aide-de-camp to General Charles Grey, observed that HMS *Somerset* and three other ships lay off the Sassafras River bordering northern Kent County while a white man and three blacks ferried back and forth to the shore in a longboat gathering provisions. Once again, this white man may have been Chalmers or one of his contacts.

Further north, George Washington was trying to gain intelligence on the enemy's approach. During his visit to the Head of Elk, Washington dined at the home of Robert Alexander on August 25, unaware that the former congressman was a loyalist. When the general asked him if he planned to stay at his home when the British arrived, Alexander replied that he had made up his mind to stay and take the consequences.[15]

Alexander did much more than "take the consequences." When General Sir William Howe came ashore, Alexander sought him out and offered his home as headquarters for the British commander. In addition, the army encamped on his grounds; in the course of six days, they devoured twenty-one of his cows, eighteen steers, eleven calves, one hundred eighteen sheep, one hundred fourteen hogs, and five hundred bushels of wheat.[16] Realizing that he could not stay in Maryland, Alexander accompanied the British when they marched.

At 9:30 A.M., Sunday, August 25, the British fleet came to anchor opposite the Cecil courthouse and the Elk ferry. The locals decided it would be interesting to watch the redcoats disembark and soon arrived as tourists. Montresor noted that the inhabitants were very numerous and "well dressed at Cecil Court House Point." The British were constantly amazed to discover that the colonists weren't always ill-clad country bumpkins. It was a preconception that lasted years after the war. Washington Irving, the first American writer to have a large international following, observed in the early 1800s that Europeans were surprised to discover an American with a feather in his writing hand rather than in his hair.

On the 26th, a heavy thunderstorm struck the Head of Elk, hindering the operation. On the 27th, Montresor noted "the storm continuing most of the morning" and that the order for marching had been countermanded. "The roads heavy.... The soldiery not sufficiently refreshed and great part of their ammunition damaged."[17]

That same day, Howe used the delay to issue a proclamation to the local population in which he assured the nervous Maryland locals that he had "issued the strictest Orders to the Troops for the Preservation of Regularity and Good Discipline, and has signified that the most exemplary Punishment shall be Inflicted upon Those who shall dare to plunder the Property, or molest the Persons of any of his MAJESTY'S Well-disposed subjects."[18]

Despite Howe's assurances, this was not completely true. While at least two were hanged and many lashed, Howe himself remitted the sentences of several soldiers caught plundering. Howe also offered pardons to anyone who had taken part in the rebellion. Few stepped forward, probably because the British came and went so quickly.

Having disembarked, the invaders marched north and entered the town of Elk at nine in the morning on August 28. Montresor noted that the town consisted of about forty well-built brick and stone houses. Only a few shots were exchanged with the rebels, who quickly fled the town and the surrounding area. They periodically harassed the outlying pickets but no large rebel forces showed themselves. After Howe set up his headquarters at Robert Alexander's home, informants entered the camp to report on a large rebel force gathered at Chadd's Ford on the Brandywine Creek in Pennsylvania. Throughout the march, the British were well informed about what lay ahead of them.

Rebel spies were busy as well. The movements of the British army were being closely monitored. Baltimore merchant Jesse Hollingsworth wrote the governor on August 29:

> I am now 4 miles North of the Enemy's Camp on the high lands above the Head of Elk. They took possession of Grays Hill 2 miles East of the Head of Elk, yesterday, and have not advanced today. Their Drums beat & a Gun was fired at Elk Point House before Day, so that I suppose their second Division to have started then from Elk ferry.... We have several Deserters, & near 100 Prisoners taken by our light Horse in Scouting Parties.[19]

During this time, James Chalmers assisted several British foraging expeditions sent out on the peninsula. Howe was very short of horses which were desperately needed to pull the artillery pieces. Chalmers later wrote that he "suggested the facility of obtaining sufficiency of horses and provisions from the fertile Counties of Cecil and Kent." He added that he "conducted detachments which in the space of two or three days, without firing a shot, did collect such sufficiency of horses, and Cattle as enabled the Army to advance."[20] Since he isn't mentioned in Howe's orders or in the journals of Montresor and André, posterity must take Chalmers at his word.

Whatever his contribution, the British army did secure horses and was soon on the move again. By September 6, less than two weeks after they first landed, the last of Howe's forces had pulled out of Elk and moved on toward Philadelphia.

The locals found their little town a bit disheveled. Despite Howe's proclamation, his men plundered at the Head of Elk. They even had the audacity to interfere with human property belonging to the rebels. William Paca complained of an additional offense to Governor Johnson:

> The Enemy have taken above seventy slaves on our Bay side and the River Elk: Upon application by some of their Masters a Day was formally appointed for a Restoration of them. When the Day came they were told they could not have them but should be paid for them on the Enemy's Return.[21]

Often, slaves were given their freedom in exchange for service to the British army. Now, homeless blacks walked beside homeless loyalists as they followed the army toward Philadelphia.

After cutting their way through the rebel position at the Battle of Brandywine, the British arrived at Germantown, a few miles northwest of Philadelphia. As the redcoats prepared for their march into the capital, the rebels did something Howe didn't expect. Despite their devastating loss at Brandywine, the rebels attacked Howe's position at Germantown. The British defeated Washington's offensive but were surprised and shaken by it. More troops were going to be needed to guard the city and its outlying areas from rebel skirmishers.

Tempted by the large numbers of potential loyal recruits that men like Philadelphia loyalist Joseph Galloway and James Chalmers were promising, Howe issued the following proclamation which appeared in the *Pennsylvania Ledger*:

> Whereas for the more speedy and effectual suppression of the unnatural rebellion subsisting in North-America, it has been thought proper to levy a number of Provincial Troops, thereby affording to his Majesty's faithful and well-disposed subjects, inhabitants of the colonies, an opportunity to co-operate in relieving themselves from the miseries attendant on anarchy and tyranny, and in restoring the blessings of peace and order with just and lawful government: As a reward for the promptitude and zeal of his Majesty's faithful subjects who may enter into the corps now raising, I DO HEREBY, in consequence of authority to me given by his Majesty, promise and engage, That all persons who have, or do hereafter inlist into any of the said Provincial Corps, to serve for two years, or during the present war in North-America, and shall continue faithfully to serve in any of the said Corps agreeable to such their engagements, shall, after being reduced or disbanded, obtain, according to their respective stations, grants of the following quantities of vacant lands in the colonies wherein their corps have been or shall be raised, or in such colony as his Majesty may think fit.
>
> Every non-commissioned officer—200 acres. Every private soldier—50 ditto.
>
> Given under my hand at Head-quarters in Germantown, this 8th Day of Oct. 1777.
>
> W. HOWE.[22]

It was hoped the notice would be very appealing to displaced loyalists arriving in the city to seek protection from the rebels. Hopes were high for a huge increase in the Provincial Corps. James Chalmers, always anxious for recognition, was going to get a loyalist regiment of his own.

The Maryland Provincial Regiment

On October 14, 1777, General "Johnnie" Burgoyne was negotiating the surrender of the British forces under his command at Saratoga, New York. It was a humiliating defeat for the British and a major turning point for the rebels.

Just to the south, British General John Vaughan was leading seventeen hundred redcoats up the Hudson River to put the rebel town of Esopus (Kingston) to the torch.

On the same Tuesday, General Smallwood wrote from the Continental's camp outside Philadelphia to Governor Johnson in Annapolis, happily informing him of "the Success of our Arms to the Northward" at Saratoga.

Just south of Philadelphia, Captain John Montresor noted the weather to be fine as he supervised the completion of a British battery on Province Island that he had started the day before.

Northwest of the city, at his headquarters in Germantown, General Sir William Howe signed his name on commissions for three new Provincial units: the Roman Catholic Volunteers, the First Battalion of Pennsylvania Loyalists, and the First Battalion of Maryland Loyalists.

Little is known about the Catholic loyalist regiment, which was under the command of Lieutenant Colonel Alfred Clifton. It was composed apparently of Roman Catholics from Delaware, Maryland, and Pennsylvania. Never a large unit, its peak strength being one hundred eighty men, the unit was dissolved by the fall of 1778 because of poor discipline. A Catholic regiment fighting for England was a very strange idea. "Papists," as they were often called, weren't allowed to join the British army. Based on that fact, it has always been assumed that Catholics invariably preferred the rebel side. Appearances may have been deceiving. One British officer being held prisoner in nearby Lancaster, Pennsylvania, noted: "Something very extraordinary, but most of the Roman Catholics are friends to [the British] Government and I believe, if an opportunity offered, would fight against those of their own religion—the French."[23]

Of those who joined the Pennsylvania loyalist regiment, only one would be remembered in the history books, the regimental chaplain, The Reverend Jonathan Odell. Odell was a close friend of New Jersey's former Royal Governor William Franklin and a writer of some note. His loyalist verses were frequently printed in Rivington's *Royal Gazette*, New York's loyalist newspaper. He would also be a key figure in the act of treason of Benedict Arnold three years later.

Heading the Pennsylvania Loyalists was Lieutenant Colonel William Allen. Early in the war, Allen had accepted an officer's commission in the Continental Army but in 1776 abandoned the cause and joined the British.[24] Coming from an influential family, he expected to raise a substantial force but was disappointed. He raised only one hundred thirty-two men, the least in numbers of the three new Provincial regiments.

The Maryland Loyalists fared far better. At their peak strength, they consisted of three hundred thirty-six rank and file troops. Although small by comparison to British regiments, Chalmers's numbers were actually as successful as many loyalist recruiting efforts. Chalmers, though, had promised a thousand men. Joseph Galloway had also told Howe of the large number of loyalists who would flock to the king's standard. Another case of loyalists offering more than they could deliver did nothing to raise their credibility level with the British high command.

A Motley Cast of Characters

One of the three captains first commissioned in the Maryland Loyalists was the Virginian Dr. Alexander Middleton. He had refused to take up arms and, like so many loyalists, was confined for a time. He fled to Philadelphia at the end of 1776 with the intention of moving on to join the British army in New York but changed his plans when he saw the appalling condition of loyalist prisoners in the rebel capital. The loyalist practitioner decided to stay and attend as best he could to the prisoners' needs.

Middleton's humanitarian gesture didn't sit well with the local rebels. According to Middleton's testimony, rebels surrounded his house one spring evening but he escaped undetected out of a window and fled into the night. He ran three miles from the city to the country home of the late John Kearsley, a Philadelphia physician. It seemed a rather conspicuous place to hide. More than a year before, Kearsley had been seized at his house by a mob of rebels who were angry with the loyalist views he espoused so loudly. He was placed in a cart and pushed through the city to the taunts and jeers of the townspeople. Kearsley, though, was defiant. He took off his wig and shook it at them with contempt. Charged with treason, he was placed in jail where he soon died after a case of insanity had set in.[25]

Middleton waited, concealed in the house by Kearsley's widow, until the British arrived in September to step out in the streets. In short order, he met up with Chalmers, got himself a captain's commission, and enrolled fifty-two men into the unit. Middleton's luck, however, was about to take a turn for the worse.

Acting as a guide for the army, he fell from his horse while pursuing rebels. His injuries were severe enough that he was forced to give up his commission and sail for England with his wife and children. He was shipwrecked on the coast of Cornwall but managed to get ashore unharmed.[26] Alexander Middleton's misfortunes were the first indication of the kind of luck that members of the Maryland loyalist regiment were going to have over the next six years.

Philip Barton Key had been studying law in Annapolis when the rebellion broke out. He allegedly refused repeated calls to sign the oath of fidelity while his brother, John Ross Key (the father of Francis Scott Key), had joined the Continentals as an officer. In August 1777, Philip Barton refused allegiance again and was not allowed to go within seven miles of navigable water. With pressure mounting, he fled to Philadelphia in December.[27]

Over the years, Philip Barton's loyalty to the Crown has come into question. There is some reason to be suspicious. When Philip Barton Key filed his claim with the British government after the war, a witness testifying in the case said Key had mustered with the Americans for a short time in 1775 (something Key hadn't mentioned) and could not recall that he had refused to sign the oath.[28]

Given the ease with which Key returned to the United States after the war, it is at least a possibility that he and his brother had made an agreement to take opposite sides in the conflict. More than a few families did such a thing not because they were each other's opponents but because they wanted to hedge their bets. Having a family member on both sides insured that, no matter who won, the losing side would not be totally at the victor's mercy. This was even more tempting if the two in question were officers. If the Americans won, a Continental officer would have the needed influence to keep his loyalist family members out of harm's way. The same would be true if the British won.

For the Sterling family of Maryland, there was no doubt about a bitter division. John and William Sterling joined the Maryland Loyalists as officers. In opposition, Henry Sterling joined the Maryland militia, while Isaac enlisted in the Second Regiment of the Maryland Continental Line. While on the Eastern Shore, Isaac actively fought against the local tories and kept the state council informed of their raids and attempts to recruit soldiers for the British army, activities during which John Sterling was one of the main culprits. Indeed, before leaving for Philadelphia, John led a raid on the home of a Somerset militia captain named David Wilson; in the fray, Wilson was shot.[29]

Irish-born Baltimore physician Patrick Kennedy had watched the war closely and made up his mind after the American victory at Trenton that the local patriots would step up their harassment of tories.[30] He fled, first to New York, then to Philadelphia, where he received one of the first captain's commissions in Chalmers's unit. Acting out Kennedy's prediction, soon after his departure from Baltimore, locals entered the doctor's office and distributed his medical supplies to the Continental Army, which was sorely lacking in such items.[31]

From western Maryland came one of that area's few loyalists. Fourteen-year-old William Augustus Bowles of Frederick Town made his way to Philadelphia with enough money to buy himself an ensign's commission in the Maryland unit. He was young, carefree, and desperately looking for adventure. As his life later showed, he wound up finding it.

Eastern Shore troublemakers Isaac Costen and Levin Townsend, both deeply involved in Eastern Shore uprisings, arrived in Philadelphia in the spring and were commissioned captain and lieutenant respectively. Caleb Jones, the former sheriff of Somerset County, soon arrived as well. Each of them brought many recruits in tow.

Perhaps aware that his officers lacked any real military experience, Chalmers obtained Lieutenant John MacDonald from the Forty-second Royal Regiment of Highlanders and managed to get him appointed major of the Maryland Loyalists.[32] Whether Chalmers and MacDonald had known each other in Scotland is uncertain.

The Reverend John Paterson, after a lengthy confinement in Baltimore County, was released in March 1778 on the condition that he mind his tongue. Paterson immediately fled to Philadelphia and Chalmers named his old pastor regimental chaplain.

Of the privates who served in the Maryland Loyalist regiment, of course, little is known. Most privates on either side couldn't write, so their legacies have been lost forever. Bits and fragments, however, are still interesting.

Some time during the regiment's stay in Philadelphia, Private Samuel Woodward of Captain Key's company married a woman named Elizabeth. The new Mrs. Woodward had already led a dramatic life. A Philadelphia native, she was first married to a sergeant in the British Marines who was stationed aboard the brig *Stanley*, a tendor to HMS *Roebuck*, which had been part of the Chesapeake fleet.

Years later, Elizabeth wrote of her exploits, which seem, to say the least, remarkable—to say the most, wildly embellished. She told of how she was wounded in her left leg in a battle aboard ship when she was actually working at the guns, making her something of a loyalist Molly Pitcher. Loyalists, however, were never very good at exploiting favorable propaganda. While Elizabeth is unknown, Molly Pitcher's alleged tending of the rebel cannon at the Battle of Monmouth is part of the fabric of the Revolution.

Elizabeth Woodward also related that when a detachment of British Marines landed at Cape May, New Jersey, her husband was taken prisoner and sentenced to death. She helped him to escape along with twenty-two American deserters. On their way back to British lines, they were attacked by a band of rebel Light Horse. "She was fired at, and wounded in her left arm; but, undismayed, took a loaded firelock, [and] shot the rebel."[33] She then took the dead man's horse with her to Philadelphia and sold it to one of Howe's aides-de-camp. At some point, her Marine husband died and she married Woodward. Amazingly, her exploits were far from over.

It was now time for the new loyalist regiments to be issued uniforms. While loyalists the year before had worn green coats, the trend now was to have the Provincials put into red coats like their counterparts, the regulars. The Maryland and Pennsylvania loyalists were issued red coats with olive-colored cuffs and lapels, known as facings. Each buttonhole was decorated with white lace.[34] The rest of their clothing most likely reflected that of the regulars: white waistcoat and breeches with black linen half-gaiters which protected their shoes and stockings from mud. Much detail of their arms and accoutrements can only be guessed at. Loyalist units frequently got the hand-me-downs from the regulars, such as older Long-Land muskets and waistbelt carriages for bayonets (which had been replaced by shoulder slings). Sometimes, getting any clothing issue was a miracle. More than a few Maryland Loyalists were still waiting for uniforms more than six months after the battalion's founding.

As word of the new loyalist regiments got out, men trickled into Philadelphia from Maryland, Delaware, and other parts of Pennsylvania to join. The numbers were small and officers were forced to take their leave to return to their respective communities and secretly try to recruit more locals. From November until the following spring, the Maryland regiment slowly built its numbers and drilled the new companies. Although they were dressed like the regulars, it still remained to be seen whether they could live up to British expectations.

4

Royal Provincials

Instead of suffering our vastly superior force to sleep in New York during four campaigns, disgracefully besieged by an undisciplined and truly contemptible enemy, let it be ordered into the field.

—Joseph Galloway, loyalist

A Winter "Holiday" in Philadelphia

When the British moved in to occupy the city, some of them were surprised at its orderly appearance, expecting a rough frontier town. Others turned their noses up at the place, feeling it fell short of their English expectations. The loyalists had little to complain about. They were just glad to be out of the reach of their rebel neighbors.

History showed the British army never left Philadelphia that winter to attack Washington at Valley Forge a short distance away. They spent most of their time tracking down rebel skirmishers on the perimeter, chopping wood, gambling, and courting the local loyalist damsels.

Robert Bell's bookstore was a popular place to visit for the officers. Bell managed to do business before and during the occupation without offending anyone which, in this war, was almost impossible. Officers and civilians made use of his circulating library and he kept a large selection of titles in stock.[1] (Presumably, copies of *Common Sense* didn't make an appearance on his shelves during this time.) The classic literature Bell carried was a reminder of home, a reminder of the finer things that were in short supply in Philadelphia.

Such a sudden influx of humanity had put a strain on the city. One order given the British and Provincial troops in Philadelphia seems to illustrate garrison life in the colonial capital better than any other:

> Notwithstanding the Great care and attention that has been paid to Render the state house Barracks particularly Clean and Comfortable, some of the men have been so beastly as to ease themselves on the Stairs and Lower area of the House between doors, the Centry is therefore in future to be very attentive (particularly during the Night) to put a stop to such scandalous behaviour and immediately to Confine any man who shall presume to make use of any other place whatever than the Privy for his Necessary Occasions. The Tubs placed within doors for the conveniency of making water during the Night are to be Emptied down the Privy every Morning immediately after gunfiring, and set in some proper place to air during the day.[2]

Soldiers in the king's service were not known for their cleanliness. Orders were constantly issued demanding the men dress properly, that they wear their neckstocks and the proper white shirt. The army demanded that the men's hair be long, tied up, and clubbed. The men, however, frequently couldn't manage to keep from looking ragged, despite the fact that they were much better supplied than the rebels less than twenty miles away at Valley Forge.

The officers were accustomed to the good life, which they pursued as best they could in the rebel capital. A number of officers decided to put together a theater schedule and Southwark Theatre at the southern end of town saw more than a dozen plays performed during the occupation. The Quaker inhabitants of the city didn't like this at all and were quick to lodge protests. They saw the theater as immoral and indecent. The British, however, paid little attention to their complaints. Theater was one of the few things that reminded the officers of London. They weren't terribly concerned with what a few stern Quakers had to say.

Some were unconcerned with what even polite society had to say. The *Pennsylvania Evening Post* ran the following personal advertisement on November 1:

> Wanted to live with two single gentlemen, a Young Woman to act in the capacity of housekeeper, and who can occasionally put her hand to anything. Extravagant wages will be given, and no character required. Any young woman who chooses to offer, may be further informed at the bar of the City Tavern.[3]

Between plays, balls, horizontal refreshments, and card games, the officers tried to party their way through the harsh winter.

However, for officers and soldiers alike, life was no picnic in Philadelphia. The winter of 1777–78 was very cold. Temperatures rarely got above freezing from Christmas to mid-March. Snow was frequent. Though they weren't housed in rude huts like Washington's men, the British and Provincial soldiers were frequently crammed into buildings left without a stick of furniture—the former rebel occupants had taken it with them as they escaped the city. When supplies of firewood were scarce, they improvised by tearing down fences or stripping unoccupied buildings of any piece of wood that could be removed. These practices, of course, were strictly prohibited by the army, but despite threats of punishment, the destruction continued.

Other problems were arising as well. Throughout the occupation, there was a degree of tension between the British regulars and the loyalist regiments. The regulars looked down on the Provincials for their lack of military experience. Yet, the British frequently didn't set a particularly good example themselves. Corporal William McSkinning of the Fifteenth Regiment attempted to murder an ensign of his unit. Found guilty and sentenced to hang, he was taken to the public place of execution with a plaque on his chest which read "Condemned for Mutiny." His body was left swinging for six hours for all to see.[4]

The Maryland Loyalists' troubles seemed mild by comparison. On May 16, General Howe's orders noted:

> Ensign John McPherson, of Maryland Loyalists, tried by the General Court Martial ordered on the 7th. instant, for ungentlemanlike behaviour; The Court are of opinion that he is not guilty, and doth therefore acquit him; and the Court are also of opinion that the facts brought to support the charge are frivolous and trifling.[5]

Patrick Mullen of the Roman Catholic Volunteers wasn't so fortunate. Discovered crossing the Schuylkill River in order to join the rebel army, he was found guilty and received a thousand lashes from a cat-o'-nine-tails.[6] The Catholics were, in fact, developing an awful reputation. Two officers were courtmartialed for plundering and a number suffered punishment similar to that of Private Mullen.

After journeying back to the Eastern Shore, loyalist troublemaker Isaac Costen arrived in Philadelphia on March 1 with nearly sixty recruits and found himself the captain of the company. Captains Caleb Jones and Philip Barton Key as well as Lieutenants Levin Townsend and John Sterling all brought in men as the winter snow began to melt.

Lieutenant Sterling later wrote he returned to Maryland "at great risque of life, at a very heavy expence, and after undergoing many dangerous difficulties, brought into Philadelphia about one hundred men."[7] Back in Maryland, the rebels were well aware of Sterling's return. His relative, Isaac Sterling, lodged a report with the council which stated, "Our Enemies have been but too successful in employing a Sett of Villains to recruit in . . . the disaffected Parts of this State."[8] In another letter, the council wished for "every Friend to the Country to get the Deserters taken up and Sterling's Recruiting put an End to."[9]

One Maryland Loyalist officer sought greener pastures. Ensign Adam Allen had recruited a number of men for Captain Alexander Middleton's company between November and January. Shortly after Middleton failed to return to service following his accident, Allen got himself transferred; he left the Maryland loyalists to become a lieutenant in the prestigious Queen's Rangers.[10]

As spring progressed, the new Provincial units were sufficiently ready to take orders for duty. On May 6, Howe ordered:

> Lieut.-Col. Allen's [Pennsylvania Loyalist] and Lieut.-Col. Clifton's [Roman Catholic] Battalions are to be in readiness to embark at the upper Coal Yard to-morrow morning at Eight with their Field Equipage and one Week's provision. Lieut.-Col. Chalmer's Battalion will be in readiness to Encamp tomorrow forenoon upon the Banks of the Schuyl-kill.[11]

Their position, as Montresor described it, was between the Upper and Middle Ferry, which put them just south of the German Jäger post west of the city. The Germans were constantly trying to get the better of Daniel Morgan's riflemen, who lingered just out of reach. The riflemen and the Germans were smart fighters and neither could draw the other into a decisive skirmish. While the Catholics and the Pennsylvania Loyalists accompanied the Fifty-fifth and Sixty-third Regiments to protect the woodcutters on the other side of the river, the Maryland Loyalists apparently had little to do. They had plenty to think about, though. Rumors were flying that the British would quit Philadelphia and return to New York.

Within a week, Howe turned over his command to Sir Henry Clinton. Sir William was going home to England after a lengthy strained relationship with Lord George Germaine, the British secretary of state for the colonies. Sensing an opportunity for advancement, Major John André decided to stage an enormous production in honor of the departing commander. The festival, named the *Meschianza*, was on such a grand scale that a number of British officers felt it a bit inappropriate in the middle of a war.

With the *Meschianza* soon over and Howe on his way back to England, the British army packed its bags and marched out of the city, leaving behind piles of filth, garbage, and excrement in the intersecting alleys. Inside houses that had been used as barracks, soldiers had cut holes in the floor and shoveled their "Sir Reverence" (an eighteenth-century euphemism for human excrement) into the basement.[12] When the rebels returned to their devastated city, they were not amused by the stench created by basements full of Sir Reverence.

A Soldier's Life

Some time in the 1800s, a Long Island family discovered a book hidden away in the attic of their house in Newtown. Upon opening its pages, they discovered it to be the orderly book of the First Battalion of Maryland Loyalists. Kept by Captain Caleb Jones, the book contains general, brigade, and regimental orders from June 18, 1778 (the day after the army left Philadelphia), to October 12, 1778 (about the time they left New York).

The house, built by settler John Moore about 1660, was regimental headquarters of the Maryland Loyalists for a time during their occupation of the island. Jones's book is the only record of the daily life of the regiment to survive. No personal observations of any kind are made but, upon examination, the collections of orders, guard details, counterorders, passwords, courtmartials, etc., paint a clear picture of the life of the Maryland Loyalist soldier.

On Friday, June 19, 1778, the British army was camped about ten miles from Philadelphia in Haddonfield, New Jersey. Security was of the highest priority. The redcoats knew the rebels would attack somewhere along the route to New York. Washington's men were well trained now, and they were ready for a fight. Even if Washington didn't engage his main force, he would certainly have riflemen hang on the flanks of the long convoy, picking off men at random and creating constant alarm. Light companies could dislodge them from their hiding places but the rebels could simply run away and re-form farther along the route. This strategy had demoralized the Brits as they returned to Boston from Concord in April of 1775. Then, they hadn't fully grasped how determined the rebel resistance was. Now, they knew and were ready for it.

Under the command of German General Wilhelm Kuyphausen, the Maryland Loyalists, usually referred to in orders as "Colo. Chalmers Corps," were grouped with the Tenth Regiment and the New Jersey Volunteers to guard the artillery baggage and provision train when the army marched out at 2 A.M. the following morning. The troops were warned "to hold themselves in readiness to march on the shortest notice" and the flanking parties to "continue till this county appear[s] open." The countersign of the day (the password given to all in camp) reflected their objective: it was simply "New York."[13]

The march proceeded across the New Jersey countryside. Loaded down with a backpack, haversack, cartridge box, bayonet, and musket, each soldier was only too aware that the heat and humidity were beginning to wear him down. To the west, Washington's army was not slowed down by an enormous baggage train. The rebel army was marching parallel to the British, threatening to overtake them and refuse their progress north. To prevent being cut off, the British columns turned east and headed for Sandy Hook.

On the 20th, the redcoat army camped at Moorestown, during which time Elisha Taylor, John Charnock, and Abel Charnock, privates in Caleb Jones's company, decided to desert.[14] The itch to go AWOL among the Marylanders increased. At Emelstown on the 24th, a sergeant and five privates were reported in the Maryland Loyalist rolls as having "Deserted to the Rebels." Similar events were happening in each regiment up and down the line.

By Thursday, June 25, Chalmers's corps marched into the town of Freehold, New Jersey, guarding the left flank of the artillery baggage train along with the Fifth and Tenth Regiments. Freehold seemed like the kind of sleepy little rural village usually forgotten by history, but this would not be the case—Washington's men were fast approaching from behind. In three days, the largest single battle of the Revolution would be fought just outside of town.

At four the following morning, the army was on the move again. Breaking up the monotony of guarding the artillery baggage was the command for "A Detachment of a 150 Men from Chalmers Corps to be in front of 4th Regiment under the Command of Coll. [Alexander] Innes." The Fourth, a royal regiment which had seen action at Concord, was part of the advance guard. Given the pecking order of the British army, which put loyalists one step in front of the horses, this command was something of an honor. Some, apparently, didn't feel too honored: Sergeant Horatio Stayten and Bryan Byrnes took their leave of the Maryland Loyalists, no doubt to join the rebels who everyone knew were closing in on the rear guard.

Lieutenant Colonel Chalmers, in addition to heading up an investigation of soldiers charged with burning houses, was ordered to form a detachment of men into what was known as "Safe Guards." This detail was charged with preventing buildings from being plundered. A number of soldiers were posted to each building to prevent stragglers from looting. By the articles of war, any soldier who challenged a safe guard on duty could find himself shot dead.[15] Chalmers was ordered to divide his safe guards into noncommissioned officer guards consisting of a sergeant or corporal and four privates, with designations of guard number 1, number 2, and so on. Once posted, they were to remain until the rear guard had passed.

At 10 A.M. on the morning of June 28, the British rear guard came under attack close to the Monmouth courthouse. (The Maryland Loyalists and Roman Catholic Volunteers, however, were more than a day's march away at Middletown. As an enormous battle waged near Freehold, Chalmers and his men sat on their hands for two days waiting for the British army to rejoin them.)

The battle was fierce yet ultimately decided nothing. Both sides fought until they were exhausted by the heat. Dozens from either side dropped dead in their tracks from heat prostration. When darkness fell, the fighting ceased. (As night fighting wasn't practical, dusk brought all such battles to a halt.) Clinton ordered his worn-out men to rest. Shortly after midnight, the British withdrew and continued on their way. The Continentals had given them a good fight but were too exhausted to give chase.

Joining Chalmers's advance guard, the army moved on to the Jersey shore. Time was taken on the third of July to hand out a little eighteenth-century military justice. Two camp followers, Elizabeth Clark and Mary Colethrate, were placed on trial for plundering. Clark was found guilty, received one hundred lashes on her bare back, and was drummed out of the army "in the Most Publick manner."[16] Apparently, being a camp follower was as rough as being a soldier in the British army.

By July 5, the march had been completed when the army reached Sandy Hook and waited to board transports to take them across Raritan Bay to New York. Captain Jones wrote in his orderly book that Clinton thanked his army for "the cherefulness which they Have Supported the fatiges of the Duty."[17] Two days later, the loyalists found themselves at Gravesend in the southern part of Long Island.

Despite their inferior status, the Maryland Loyalists were occasionally given a small degree of respect. As the unit waited for orders, ten men of the regiment were detached to Clinton's personal guard detail and three others to guard Sir William Erskine, the quartermaster general who now commanded the eastern district of Long Island.[18] Such honors would be few, as the Marylanders were soon to discover.

With the arrival of the troops on Long Island, the army attempted to stop the burning of every fence in sight. Orders were constantly issued *not* to burn fences or plunder. With the rebels at a safe distance, they could try to improve the bearing of the soldiers as well. On July 13, the Maryland Loyalists were told:

> The Battalion to Parade at troop Beating [the drum call for assembly] Every Morning for Exercize.... The Orderly Corporal to Parade their men and the awkward men of their Respective Companys and assist the Drill Sergeant in Teaching them no man to appear on a Parade or beyond the Sentreys of the Battalion without being uniformly Dressed.... No man of What Ever Rank to Leave the Camp without proper Leave. No Man to take his fire Lock [musket] to Pieces.[19]

As Chalmers would later admit, he expected that his regiment would now be involved in raids into Connecticut. It would give his regiment a chance to prove itself to the British, something which certainly hadn't happened yet. Chalmers had good reason to believe they would be utilized for battle. After all, their expedition was being commanded by Major General William Tryon who had led a raid into Connecticut just the year before and succeeded in burning the town of Danbury to the ground. Chalmers probably didn't give much thought to the fact that the 1777 raid had been accomplished by British regulars. The British high command, to Chalmers's chagrin, had other plans for the new Provincial units.

On July 22, Major General Tryon, who had the unusual distinction of having served as royal governor of North Carolina *and* New York, issued the following orders: "Lt. Collo. Chalmers Battalion to march Early to morrow morning and Encamp Near Jamacea and on friday will Proceed by force Marches to huntington Where they Will Encamp and Waitt there for further orders. The strictest Discipline will be Maintained."[20]

The tents were struck at 3:30 A.M. and the Maryland Loyalists marched out at 4:00. They were now on the move every day, escorting two artillery fieldpieces. By Friday, July 31, they had reached Huntington, perched on Huntington Bay. Twelve miles across Long

Island Sound was the Connecticut shoreline, its inhabitants in daily expectation of being raided, as had happened the year before. The Marylanders camped and waited for orders.

One of the very few clues about the clothing provisions of the Maryland Loyalists was recorded on the following day. A return was requested showing the number of men in Chalmers's regiment who had not received clothing, presumably regimental redcoats. Although no firsthand description appears to exist regarding their general appearance, it's probable some of the men may have been wearing the clothes they enlisted in, or perhaps some were given the older issue green loyalist coats.

Any hope of a go at the Connecticut rebels faded when the Marylanders and the Roman Catholic Volunteers pulled up tent stakes and moved on the following morning. They headed east to Smithtown, then to Setauket overlooking the sound where the quarter guards were told to furnish "a Sentry towards the water side from hence all Boats are to Be Drawn up so they are not Liable to be landed without the nowligee [knowledge] of the sentry."[21]

They continued east to Wading River where it was noted "the General [Tryon] is so Sorrey to have Occation to Take Notise of the Sorrey Scanderlus and Irregular Behaver of Some Disorderly Soldiers."[22] Who this referred to is unclear. Given the bad reputation of the Roman Catholic Volunteers, they may have been the object of the general's comments.

This lack of discipline is understandable under the circumstances. They were nearing the eastern edge of Long Island, a good week's march from New York City and civilization. Paroles (the passwords given to officers of the guard) and countersigns, which had been changed daily on the march from Philadelphia, were now left unchanged for days or even weeks at a time. They were in the middle of nowhere without the slightest danger of being attacked by the rebel army. Any group of irregular militia that presented itself would be no threat to such a large expeditionary force.

On August 8, they reached their objective, the town of Mattituck on Peconic Bay. They would remain until the 24th, engaged in the service of their king. The British had sent them marching from one side of Long Island to the other in order to act as cattle guards. The British officers in New York City would need these provisions if they were going to get through another season of theatrical productions.

The business of escorting cattle apparently didn't sit well with the Maryland Loyalists. During the two weeks the unit spent at Mattituck, twenty-four members of the regiment deserted. These events were observed in the rebel newspapers as well. On August 26, the *New Jersey Gazette* observed:

> We are informed that General Tryon, with a detachment of troops from New York, has lately been on the East end of Long Island, plundering and driving off all the cattle in that quarter; and that in this excursion he had lost a great number of his men by disertion; who, after they had deserted, hid themselves in woods and bye places, in order to embrace every opportunity in coming over to the Main, which had been greatly facilitated by our people sending boats over for that purpose.[23]

General Tryon tried to shift the blame away from the soldiers. On August 10, Caleb Jones noted:

> Gen. Tryon has Received Information that Some Disofected Inhabitants on Long Island have by Base and fowl Insiniation addressed to With Draw the affections of the Soldiers from the Sollom Ingagement they have entered into to Support the Honnor of his Majesteys Crown and Happy Constitution of the County by encouraging them to Dissert.[24]

It's doubtful the soldiers could have been persuaded to desert if they hadn't already wanted to. Tryon tried to make the best of a losing situation. The record showed he wasn't too successful.

On Tuesday, August 25, the Maryland Loyalists, Roman Catholics Volunteers, the First and Third Battalions of De Lancey's Brigade, and a large group of undisciplined cattle headed west in the direction they had come. Jones noted: "On Account of the Great heat of The Day and the Driness of the march, the General has thought proper to Order Each man A Guill of Rum which the Officers are Desired to see it mixed with a Proportion of Water."[25]

This was a fairly common occurrence. When the soldiers were under undue strain, issues of rum made the day's work a bit more bearable. Given their scanty diets, the rum probably worked its effects quite nicely.

By September 5, the brigade had reached Flushing, where the Maryland Loyalists remained for more than a month. The quartermaster general, no doubt extremely embarrassed by the scores of desertions which had occurred on the expedition, tried to put yet another spin on the subject by saying the deserters had left not because they doubted their cause but because they simply missed their families. He tried to remind the troops to keep their honor and remember their duty so as not to return to their families in disgrace.

With little to do once more, the men looked for other ways to occupy their time. An order was soon given for the captain of the day to arrest soldiers who were selling liquor in camp. The liquor was to be "secured" (which probably meant it wound up on the officers' table that evening).

On September 13, a number of prisoners were executed or put under the lash. Private Peter Brown of Captain Jones's company was given five hundred lashes for attempting to desert. This sentence, horrifying as it may be, was typical for such an offense. When punishments were administered, every soldier was assembled on the parade ground to witness the event. It was cruel but effective; after this date, the number of desertions dropped off dramatically.

Days dragged by with nothing to do. Lieutenant John Sterling of Frisby's company was sent into New York with a sergeant to recruit soldiers and pick up any stragglers that may have wandered into town. By all appearances, the high command had little real use for the Marylanders.

About this time, it was announced that the Pennsylvania and Maryland Loyalists would be sent to British West Florida to fight Britain's other enemy: Spain. Earlier in the year, rebel Captain James Willing had led a raid down the Mississippi River, destroying British property at a great rate. Florida was being dragged into the conflict even though Spain wasn't officially allied to the United States.

Now, England was going to defend its Florida holdings. The news didn't go over terribly well with the Maryland Provincials: Lieutenants John Boswell and Thomas Parker resigned in short order.

As the unit reluctantly prepared to depart, Lieutenant Colonel Chalmers had a political issue to settle. On October 27, he wrote Clinton:

> Your Memorialist begs leave to observe to Your Excellency that Sir Wiliam Howe granted Commissions date October 14th 1777 to Lieut. Col. Allen and to Your Memorialist.
> Wherefore, if the Pensylvania & Maryland Loyalists serve together, their rank will be in contest.
> Your Memorialist, Sir, humbly hopes that he has not been inattentive to the spirit of his appointment; and with the utmost diffidence would suggest that Lieut. Colo. Allen, claiming no greater military experience and being many years younger than Your Memorialist, can hardly expect to command him.[26]

Despite Chalmers's attempt to settle the matter, the bickering concerning the identity of the ranking Provincial officer continued long after the troops landed in Florida. Chalmers's agenda, however, went far beyond his rank. For more than a year, he had plotted to change the course of the war—all by himself.

5

A Cunning Plan

His excessively refined affability, in general, appeared precisely what Frenchmen have denominated "la bonne politesse de la vielle cour" (the refined manners of the old nobility).
—*Gentleman's Magazine*, London 1806, speaking of James Chalmers

Convincing the British army to make one a lieutenant colonel in charge of one's very own regiment would have been enough for most loyalists. They were happy just to have someplace to go after seeing their homes confiscated. Chalmers, however, wanted more—much more. If any British generals had listened to him, Chalmers might have wound up in everyone's history books.

His plotting started more than a year before his regiment left for Florida. As early as September 28, 1777, several weeks before receiving his officer's commission, Chalmers wrote to Sir William Howe. The British army had marched into Philadelphia only two days before, barely enough time for Sir William to decide where to put his drinks cabinet. The British generals and their chief engineer, Captain Montresor, were still surveying the lay of the land to determine where they should build fortifications when the Maryland loyalist drew up his thoughts on pressing matters.

First and foremost, he wanted to establish the fact that he was receiving intelligence from informants: "I am informed by respectable

Quakers just arrived from Kent and Cecil Countys that tho' every species of falsehood had been practiced on the Simplicity of the Inhabitants few assembled as Militia and those generally dispersed in a short time."[1]

It's no accident that he spoke so highly of Quakers in *Plain Truth*. Chalmers knew it was not a good idea to be critical of people he was using as spies. In all probability, he neglected to mention to the Quakers (who were well known for their abolitionist views) that he was a slave-owner. To Chalmers, this was a minor point since many of the Americans he was plotting against also owned slaves.

Chalmers had a plan. Namely, invade the Eastern Shore, occupy it, and effectively cut the colonies in two. He wouldn't be the first or last to suggest such an idea. Robert Alexander was another influential Marylander who mentioned a similar plan. Chalmers, however, probably knew the local economy, the people, and the terrain better than any other loyalist with the British army: "It would be satisfactory to His Majesty and the British Nation to find nearly one twelfth part of the American Subjects without bloodshed return to their duty."[2]

The Maryland loyalist believed in his plan. As the months progressed, as Howe left and Sir Henry Clinton took his place as commander in chief, the lieutenant colonel continued to lobby for his scheme. Each time he made his proposal, the planning became more intricate; more details were elaborated on; and greater intelligence from spies came into play.

"Begging Pardon for This Freedom"

On Friday, July 24, 1778, a month after the battle of Monmouth, Chalmers took up his quill while encamped at Huntington on Long Island and wrote Clinton. He penned a "memorial," an eighteenth-century equivalent of a resume. One senses he was trying quite hard to establish his credentials to the new leader with whom, unlike Howe, he had had no conversations. Chalmers, ever proud of his own work, included complimentary copies of *Plain Truth* and *Additions to Plain Truth* with the letter. He told Clinton it contained "many bold truths & displayed ardent zeal to His Sovereign." He then added that he "humbly imagines that in one of said Pamphlets; he [Clinton] has glanced at certain measures to be pursued by England in War with perfidious France." History doesn't record if Sir Henry ever read *Plain Truth* or the sequel.

Chalmers detailed his previous service to the British during the landing at the Head of Elk. Mentioning that he had nearly completed raising his regiment, he couldn't resist adding that he did so despite the fact that his property and province were "inaccessible." Furthermore, he didn't hesitate to add "few Provincial Officers have relinquished more."[3]

This "memorial" to the new commander in chief was unique in that Chalmers refrained from detailing his plans for the Eastern Shore of Maryland. He may have hoped to present them in person as he had done with Howe. It's also likely that he was uncertain how his unit would be used by the British once they reached New York. As already mentioned, he expected his unit to see action in the north. When that didn't happen and he watched his men doing little more than herding cattle, he decided to push his ideas to Clinton.

From camp at Flushing Fly on September 12, over a year after penning the "memorial," Chalmers wrote his first letter detailing his intentions. He was taking extraordinary liberties—the idea of a Provincial officer having any sort of influence with the British high command was almost unheard of. Only a select few loyalists like Joseph Galloway and Robert Alexander had gained the ear of the commander in chief, but they were civilians. Chalmers was presenting not only intelligence but a plan to win the war—his plan. Perhaps in an effort to stem criticism for overstepping his bounds, Chalmers began by telling Clinton that he hoped his ideas "will be considered by your

Excellency as the reveries of a good subject rather than the speculations of a Visionary."[4]

In a subsequent letter, he was again concerned for his credibility with the commander:

> Having seen and reflected much on the present Rebellion, I am well aware of the danger of proposing speculations flowing from an over sanguine or heated imagination. No! Sir, I can refer you to many judicious persons who can corroborate the simple truths here enumerated.[5]

Having done this, he was entirely prepared to plot a course for the entire war. Dismissing Rhode Island and New York as nothing more than arsenals, the lieutenant colonel argued that possession of the extensive and fertile lands between Delaware and the Chesapeake Bay had yet to be regarded with the urgency he felt was necessary.

He set his sights on two key locations for effectively blockading the rebels: first, Port Penn, strategically located at the first narrow spot on the Delaware River. Once in range, ships could not pass it without facing blistering cannon fire from shore batteries; thus the fort effectively blockaded Philadelphia by sea. To complement this position, Chalmers suggested occupying the town of Oxford at the mouth of the Choptank River in Maryland.[6] Though a small town today, during the Revolution Oxford was one of Maryland's busiest ports, giving fierce competition to Annapolis and Baltimore. It was a vital link to Washington's troops, being a shipping point for the army's provisions. Chalmers was undoubtedly aware that, despite its importance, it wasn't particularly well guarded. In addition to severely curtailing shipments of provisions across the Chesapeake, occupying Oxford would put a fleet of British ships within easy striking distance of prosperous Annapolis.

Still convinced the British were intending to push north in the spring campaign, he contended "a Small armament sent to Chesapeak, would produce happy—nay glorious consequences." The sites to be conquered naturally would have to include "the most seditious Town of Baltimore," its prosperous shipping and numerous granaries being irresistible targets. Also ripe for burning were the stores of provisions at the Head of Elk and nearby Charlestown, a task which he insisted could be accomplished "by a handfull of Troops."[7]

Here was a key point in Chalmers's eyes. "These stores are of the *first* consequence to the Rebel Army," he stated emphatically.[8] Chalmers wouldn't have forgotten how frantically the rebels had evacuated their stores at Elkton as the British fleet approached a year earlier.

A further suggestion was, in hindsight, perhaps the most astute of all. Chalmers predicted that rebel spies would exaggerate the number of British troops engaged in the suggested operation, thereby causing the local militia to lie low and not take the field. "In such case, Washington must greatly weaken his Army or suffer this Country to be retained by the King's Troops."

Chalmers was also betting that the rebels would be fearful that the British would invade Virginia from their new base of operations on the Eastern Shore. He added, "Williamsburg may securely be destroyed tho' Washington has, it is generally believed, pledged Himself to haste to the relief of that his Province."[9] With that, he signed his name to the page.

All of this was really just a tease. Trying to get Clinton to rise to his bait, Chalmers was undoubtedly hoping for a face-to-face meeting to discuss his ideas at length. Chalmers wasn't finished with his plan; in fact, he was just getting started.

As the regiment he raised struggled to build fortifications in British West Florida in July 1779, Chalmers was in the British stronghold of New York City. Why he was there is still something of a mystery. One of the only surviving clues is contained in a letter Sir Henry Clinton wrote to Major General John Campbell in Pensacola on August 12 saying, among other things, that "Colonel Chalmers shall have my leave to remain here as long as his Occasions require."[10] What those "Occasions" entailed was never stated.

CHALMERS'S PLOT THICKENS

Whatever else he may have been doing, Chalmers was still busy drawing up yet another presentation concerning the Eastern Shore of Maryland. By now, he was fighting an uphill battle. The British had already begun their southern campaign, capturing Savannah, Georgia, with ease in December 1778. Now, they had their eyes on Charleston, South Carolina. It would be nearly impossible to redirect the war department's attention to a different strategy. This time, Chalmers put everything he could think of into the equation. In the space of eight closely written pages and over seventeen hundred words, the Maryland loyalist again made his proposal.

He put forth his theory about the character and disposition of the inhabitants of the Eastern Shore by first citing what he saw as the unique situation of the Maryland colony.

> Perhaps it may not be important to observe that, in the Constitution of Maryland, Lord Baltimore adopted & retained more of the Monarchial Government than did the Legislators of any other of the English Colonies. This excellent policy was ever signally conspicious in the superior rigour of the laws & good government of Maryland untill overwhelmed in the present rebellion.
> The Original Colonists were principally English & Irish, Romanists [Roman Catholics] or of the English Church . . . [They] are perhaps more *interested* and better disposed to remain British Subjects than any other People of America.[11]

It is remarkable to realize that Chalmers viewed his former neighbors in such dispassionate, Machiavellian terms. In his mind, these people were just subjects—pawns—to be manipulated in whatever fashion best suited the British army. They weren't to be trusted, merely exploited if things turned in England's favor.

All pledges to king and country aside, Chalmers wasn't against making a fat pile of cash out of the war himself. When he said that "the produce of Refugies Estates from the Peninsula would perhaps supply with provisions a Body of troops sufficient to defend the Isthmus," he was including his own farmlands and, no doubt, those of Kent County friends like James Frisby in the bargain. *Someone* would have to make a fortune selling provisions to the British army; why not those who had risked everything for their loyalty to good King George?

Repeating the value of an occupied upper Chesapeake, Chalmers laid out the appeal of attacking Virginia from this position. Virginia, he said, consisted of extensive plantations "chiefly cultivated by Slaves who detest their Masters." He saw Virginia as weak: "A good Officer with 2 or 3000 Men could ravage & force to submission a considerable part of Virginia & perhaps liberate the remains of G[eneral] Burgoyne's troops."[12]

A majority of the British troops in question were to be found up the Potomac River at Fort Frederick. Built during the French and Indian War to protect the western frontier against Indian attacks, the abandoned stone fort near Big Pool, Maryland, was refurbished after the British surrender at Saratoga and put in order to serve as a prison for Burgoyne's soldiers. It did not enjoy a very good reputation among the redcoats: Ensign Thomas Hughes of the Fifty-third Regiment spoke of Fort Frederick in his journal, referring to it as "the most dismal place by the description that can be imagin'd, it being environ'd by a pine swamp."[13] Holed up in the remote fort, the British and German prisoners had been nearly forgotten. An early "release" of these troops would certainly have changed the theater of war in Virginia.

Chalmers could foresee a grand plan where "every town from the entrance of Cheasapeak to the Susquehanak would be liable to assured destruction."[14] The Maryland capital, Annapolis, could be destroyed by just five hundred men and the town of Baltimore "reduced" by fifteen hundred men without loss. As an added bonus, Chalmers indicated his willingness to take part by stating he'd be happy to act with either detachment. This particular point he would pursue more aggressively later on.

Pennsylvania was mentioned as an important area to bring under British control—an action which neither Howe nor Clinton had seriously pursued. Bands of Indians and green-coated Butler's Rangers had ravaged Wyoming Valley around Wilkes-Barre just the year before. These actions, however, did little more than provide the rebels all of the raw material they needed for effective propaganda. Phrases like "ruthless savages" and "their brutal tory allies" were filling up whig newspapers.

Chalmers, though, didn't see Pennsylvania as any kind of strategic stronghold. He looked at the state through the eyes of an economist and decided that thriving towns like Lancaster should be captured and exploited for their industry. From the same economic perspective, he viewed holding the peninsula in British hands essential in cutting off trade to America's new ally, France. He was quick to doubt any philosophical motives for France joining the rebels:

> The tobacco commerce doubtless was one of the principal motives which incited France to Her perfidious measures.... By occupying the Peninsula, it is apprehended that much property of France would fall into the Captors' hands and that Her commerce would receive a Most capital injury by being deprived of Cheasapeak.[15]

Citing a 1,200 percent rise in tobacco prices in Europe, he saw the French enthusiasm for the rebellion languishing, if their one true incentive in the war—profit—was taken away.

In guarded language, he criticized the British commander's decision to set his sights on the Carolinas and Georgia:

> The maritime situation & other circumstances of the Peninsula rendor it more capable of being defended & preserved by Great Britain than any country of equal extent & goodness in America.... Maturely considering every circumstance, I am warranted to assert that this possession is of more real consequence to Great Britain than Carolina.[16]

Here, he drew an important distinction between the Eastern Shore of Maryland and the Carolinas: The British could hold onto the Chesapeake and inflict considerable economic punishment. The eventual conquest of a place like Charleston might look good in the London newspapers but would do little to actually win the war. The benefits of the Eastern Shore were quite numerous in Chalmers's mind:

> The Rebels will scarce have a port from Ocracoke, N[orth] Carolina to New London [Connecticut]; and it is not improbable but that the utter depreciation of their currency and Washington's distress for provisions may be numbered amongst the just fruits of this possession.
>
> Many good reasons favour the opinion that a post in the Isthmus, as it were in the very bowels of the Rebellion, would be a judicious measure, even if commanding Cheasapeak and securing 8 or 9000 Square Miles of valuable territory were objects of much less importance than they really are.[17]

He was now telling Sir Henry that if only one post were to be retained in America, the Delmarva Peninsula would be the "proper location" for anyone acquainted with the country in question.

What would his plan mean in terms of manpower? Chalmers proposed 5,000 infantry and a small contingent of dragoons or mounted rangers. If Clinton chose option B, possession of the isthmus only, without pillaging and plundering the next-door neighbors, a mere 2,000 soldiers would do the trick. Earlier, he had suggested 1,000 men as sufficient (under his command, of course). In addition, a large frigate should cruise back and forth across the Bay between Annapolis and the Sassafras River along the northern border of Kent County. This would effectively stop provisions (and potential rebel recruits) from Virginia and North Carolina from finding their way north via the Eastern Shore.

He also made reference to the military actions of British General Edward Mathew. Mathew had led a very successful raid into Virginia just two months prior to Chalmers's current letter. On May 9, he and his troops had invaded Hampton Roads and moved unopposed through Portsmouth, Norfolk, Gosport, and Suffolk, seizing large quantities of military and merchant goods. Chalmers made note of the fact that, as this was happening, Baltimoreans had tried in vain to raise a militia and, worried about a possible attack by water, had removed their vessels as well as those of the French to the safety of the Chester River near Chalmers's old home town. Possessing the Eastern Shore would, of course, put an end to all this sort of nonsense. The rebels would essentially have no place to hide any longer.

The Maryland loyalist was also very confident of other loyal citizens still living on the Eastern Shore to give great support to the British should they move in for occupation. While this made perfect sense to him, it's doubtful Clinton or any other British general would have been very convinced of Chalmers's assertion. With relatively few exceptions, the British held the loyal colonists at arm's length. The English doubted their commitment and questioned their dependability, certain that their loyalties shifted from moment to moment depending on who was making a better offer. Some colonists did play the two sides against each other; but a large number, at least on the Eastern Shore, were loyal yet fearful of reprisals if they spoke up. Most of the more outspoken Maryland loyalists were men of property and influence. The Maryland government knew who they were as well and worked very hard to silence them. Realizing they would have been hanged or sent to jail, many of these men had journeyed to Philadelphia and joined the Maryland Loyalist regiment as officers.

> On approach of the King's Troops, the very few violent Rebels would confide in the King's clemency or fly the peninsula.... In all or most of the Counties, a Militia may be established to preserve internal tranquility.... I do verily believe that with proper attention, a Body of men may be levied to assist in defence of the Isthmus; provided, they are assured of serving that end only.[18]

This last point may have been perfectly natural to a Maryland planter like Chalmers but the concept of negotiating the terms of service with colonists generally irritated the British. After all, this bold sort of individualism had started the rebellion in the first place. In retrospect, the whole situation becomes even more unusual when one remembers that the British commander in chief had spent a good part of his youth in New York. Whether or not Clinton understood the Americans, Chalmers faced one great potential obstacle: he had been commissioned by Sir William Howe, and Clinton openly despised Howe's ability and judgment. Whatever privilege Chalmers had enjoyed with Howe, it's questionable if he was on the same footing with Clinton.

After this letter, Chalmers disappeared from view until the following spring, when he showed up with Clinton's forces at Charleston. Eighty-five hundred British troops began an attack on the city on April 13. Though we know that, within a week, Clinton had advanced his siege lines to within two hundred yards of the American defenses, how Chalmers came to take part in this military operation is a complete mystery. (Even in his memorial to the British government in 1784, though Chalmers mentioned his presence at Charleston, he never said what he was doing there.)

The only trace of his time in South Carolina consists of two letters sent to John André, Clinton's deputy adjutant general (who would be hanged as a spy by Washington in the aftermath of Benedict Arnold's defection in October). On April 26, Chalmers sent André a brief message and a copy of a letter he had sent to Lord Rawdon concerning strategies of war involving British West Florida and the West Indies. Perhaps, he could have simply handed it to Clinton, but Chalmers had probably ascertained that André was a young officer being groomed for top rank in the British army; at twenty-nine, André was capable, ambitious, and open to new ideas. Still, Chalmers was stepping on eggshells by sending the unsolicited advice. He fawningly wrote, "I know . . . that You will rather impute this freedom to Zeal than indiscretion."[19]

By mid-May, the Americans had surrendered the city to Clinton. On the 31st, Chalmers contacted André again to say that the commander in chief had ordered him back to New York. When Major William Erskine, Clinton's quartermaster general, gave up his post and returned to England, Chalmers assumed some of his duties resolving rents to be paid for houses the army was using in the city.[20] But this was hardly going to satisfy Chalmers for long.

Clinton had also returned to New York about this time. On July 21, Chalmers's letter-writing campaign began again. Little new was covered in the first letter; much was restated from previous correspondence. Again, he reinforced just how economically important the Eastern Shore was, complete with estimates of production of wheat, lumber, and the like. Chalmers gave a complete assessment of the islands in the Chesapeake Bay with indications of their size and what type of crops were being harvested. "These Islands are all accessible to a Frigate or two who would overmatch all the Rebel naval force of (the) Cheasapeak. They afford good anchorage as does all or most parts of that Bay."[21]

It wasn't until the fall that Chalmers geared up for one last attempt at influence. He knew the armies in the field would be in winter quarters for several months, and during this slow time, the British generals would be deciding strategy for the spring of 1781. On October 13, 1780, came Chalmers's last strategy letter. He again cited the agricultural advantages of his old residence:

> It may truly be said to produce more wheat at present than all the rest of the Revolted Colonies. . . . The Rebel Armies & Northern Colonies last year would have hardly existed independent of this Country, the considerable produce of which is so easily transported by the Delaware. . . .[22]

He cited a letter from General Washington written in April concerning the great lack of flour in the army's provisions and the terrible situation of the troops. The Congress had forwarded this message to the leaders of Maryland in hopes of alleviating the situation. It's unknown how Chalmers obtained this intelligence. It does, however, illustrate that for a man who seems to have been behind British lines for nearly three years, Chalmers had a very good idea of what was happening in his native Maryland. The crop yields of his rebel neighbors were frequently listed in his letters. When an Eastern Shore county succeeded or failed in enlisting recruits for a local militia, Chalmers always knew about it. Although one of his chief contacts, William Slubey, had already been identified to the state council in the summer of 1779, other informers apparently took his place undetected.

That his suggestions were falling on deaf ears and his credibility was being called into question seems to show in Chalmers's tone:

> That the disposition of the People of the Peninsula is very generally favourable to restoration of order cannot be doubted—nor does this information flow from interested motives or an overheated imagination—it is founded deliberately on rational circumstantial & unequivocal proofs.[23]

Obviously, the British were slow to agree. Although their warships entered the Bay many times, no master plan like the one Chalmers had been suggesting for so long had ever been seriously considered. The British had been willing to land on the Eastern Shore occasionally to trade for salt or other commodities, but they did little in their brief stays to encourage any sort of sweeping loyalist support among the locals. There was an indication now, however, that Clinton *had* read Chalmers's letters. What's more, he was ready to put the plan into operation.

"A Very Intelligent Friend of Ours"

The following spring, the British moved through the Carolinas into Virginia. Their victories were as frequent as their losses but they were losing men they couldn't possibly replace.

Correspondence between Clinton, Lieutenant-General Earl Cornwallis, and Major-General William Phillips suddenly began to mention the "Upper Chesapeak" more and more often. In a letter dated April 26, 1781, Clinton told Phillips at Petersburg of a plan that sounds very familiar.

> There is in my humble opinion still another operation, which if successful would be most solidly decisive in its consequences, and is therefore well worth our consideration.... Virginia has been in general looked upon as universally hostile; Maryland has not been as yet tried, but it is supposed to be not quite so much so: but the inhabitants of Pennsylvania on both sides of the Susquehannah, York, Lancaster, Chester, and the Peninsula between Chesapeak and Delaware, are represented to me to be friendly. There or thereabouts, I think this experiment should now be tried, but it cannot be done fairly until we have a force sufficient not only to go there, but to retain a respectable hold of the country afterwards, should it be judged necessary. I wish that our numbers were competent to the occupying two corresponding stations at Baltimore and Elk river.[24]

Everything connected to Clinton's plan had a "Chalmers" sound to it, particularly his suggested ports of conquest like Port Penn and Oxford, ideas put forth by Chalmers two years before. Clinton mentioned having had several conversations with Phillips on this subject in the past:

> I have now the greater reason to be convinced that the opinions I then gave you were right, from a conversation I have since had with a very intelligent friend of ours from the country, known to Colonel Simcoe, who goes to you by this opportunity, and will be able to give you the fullest information thereon.[25]

This friend isn't identified, although it was most likely Chalmers or Robert Alexander, Marylanders who knew the land better than anyone else of equal status in the British service. Regardless, however, of who went, he had the misfortune of traveling to meet a dead man: Phillips expired of typhoid fever in May, at least a week before the letter would have reached his hands.

Just five months later, the British were trapped at Yorktown, Virginia, and forced to surrender. Clinton blamed Cornwallis for the defeat. Cornwallis, in turn, blamed Clinton.

Chalmers, the Revolutionary War strategist, had come amazingly close to seeing his plans put into action. Suddenly, he was left without a purpose. His regiment had recently returned from West Florida. Unfortunately, there was little cause for rejoicing.

6

Fighting the Spanish

Irish vagabonds who from natural fickleness and instability of their disposition, which has been confirmed by their late roaming way of life, would desert without any other temptation.

—General John Campbell
(speaking of the Maryland Loyalists)

War, Politics, War

At the end of the French and Indian War in 1763, West Florida fell into the hands of the British. It was all a part of typical postwar bargaining. Spain gave West Florida to England. In return, the British gave back Havana, which they had been so rude as to capture from the Spanish. This acquisition gave England a port on the Gulf of Mexico which they could protect, if necessary, with warships.

When the Revolution began, the local inhabitants were far removed from the fighting in the north. But tensions were on the rise because of disagreements with the Spanish neighbors in Louisiana over the use of the Mississippi River. Another problem was the royal governor, Peter Chester. From the time he took office in 1770, he didn't get along well with the assembly. A power struggle between the two ended when he dissolved the body in 1772 after a dispute arose over election procedures. James Chalmers apparently wasn't impressed with the governor.

He wrote, "Twice have the Colonists prayed the King to remove Governor Chester whose age they alege disqualifys him for Government."[1]

The bigger picture wasn't looking good for King George either. At the outbreak of the Revolution, Spain and France both had scores to settle with England. France was soon allied to the United States. The British knew they would eventually have to fight the Spanish; it was only a matter of time. In the aftermath of a rebel raid in 1778, it was decided to reinforce the neglected posts at Pensacola and St. Augustine.

"I Am Now in the Worst Part of the World"

By the end of October 1778, the Maryland Loyalists had been shipped out of New York City. In a word, they were expendable. As Clinton wrote, "For those garrisons [at Pensacola and St. Augustine] I have employed foreign troops and provincials, whose loss to this army will not be so much felt."[2] In hindsight, he was dead wrong. In two years' time, Lieutenant-General Cornwallis would have been able to put three thousand men to very good use in the Carolinas.

Apparently, the Provincials weren't keen to go to West Florida. Edward Winslow, the muster master general of provincial forces, noted loyalist hesitation to follow unpopular orders and wrote on November 13:

> The sending [of] Provincial Troops on such services has become [a] matter of consideration among 'em; they have generally censured the measure as unjust & not consistent with the original compact. This assertion arises from an idea that all or most of the provincial corps were Local & intended to defend particular provinces from which they could not be removed but by their own consent. Contracted as this sentiment may at first appear there is some reason for it.... Most of the recruits enlisted expressly for the term of two years, or during the continuance of the rebellion; there is not wanting among them men of sufficient cunning

to suggest that those terms imply an option in the soldier whether he will continue in service after the expiration of the first period; quibbling and dishonorable as this suggestion may seem to a European gentleman; it is a tolerable pretence for an American labourer.[3]

Winslow didn't see this as a good thing. He acknowledged that many loyalists had joined to gratify revenge for "recent persecutions and injuries" but that the initial rush of excitement had worn off as the cold reality of army life set in. What made matters even worse for the men were the officers of the Provincial line. Winslow declared most of them to be "Coxcombs"—superficial pretenders to knowledge—which had made the Provincial rank and file "miserable and unhappy." Although he didn't single out any one regiment, he also didn't exempt any Provincial units from this general description. So, it was a boat of these miserable and unhappy loyalists who were shipped south to fight the other British enemy—Spain.

The fleet docked in Jamaica and stayed for weeks as the ships underwent repairs and took on provisions. When they sailed for Pensacola at the end of December, the Maryland Loyalists brought an uninvited guest with them—smallpox. Even before they sailed, Captain Grafton Dulany had already died from the dreaded disease.[4] Though the other regiments were affected as well, the Marylanders suffered most.

By the end of January 1779, the troops had landed at their new quarters in British West Florida. None were very impressed. Hugh Mackay Gordon, the deputy muster master general and deputy inspector of Provincials, proclaimed, "You may easily conceive what a change coming from a pleasant, plentiful comp[any] into a most wretched one and I may say with safety I am now in the worst part of the world."[5] The chaplain of the German Waldeck Regiment called it "a desolate, uncultivated, waste . . . wholly cut off from the world."[6]

The Marylanders were now in a desperate state. As soon as they came ashore, men began dying. The companies of Captains Isaac

Costen and Caleb Jones were the hardest hit. From January to the end of February, Costen lost seventeen men while Jones lost twelve.[7] To make matters worse, the regiment was having other problems as well.

General John Campbell, the commandant at Pensacola, was not impressed by the shipment of Provincials. He noted that the Maryland and Pennsylvania Loyalists arrived in "tatters and rags instead of uniforms" and described them as "composed of the greater part of Irish vagabonds [deserters from the rebels] who from natural fickleness and instability of their disposition, which has been confirmed by their late roaming way of life, would desert without any other temptation."[8] What a surprise it would be for Campbell to learn he was mistaken in his impression.

While the Marylanders were unable to muster due to the smallpox, the Pennsylvania Loyalists did turn out their men. This, in turn, created a political problem. Campbell was ready to give Lieutenant Colonel Allen preference in the command structure should the two units be merged. Tensions were running high between Chalmers and his Pennsylvania rival, Allen.

In the midst of this regimental bickering, Ensign William Augustus Bowles resigned his commission on March 28. His reasons weren't fully explained. He apparently insulted a superior officer, perhaps the captain of his company, Patrick Kennedy. The impulsive young Bowles then tossed his regimental coat into the bay and joined a group of Lower Creek Indians who had come to Pensacola in search of presents. Bowles traveled with them for a short time but became restless and headed back toward Pensacola. In a makeshift boat, he spent his days fishing and hunting in the bay with "the sky his canopy and the earth his bed." After free-loading off a baker in Pensacola, Bowles encountered the Creeks again and once more left with them for adventure.

In a short time, he was living on the Chattahoochee River, where he married a Cherokee girl. His wife gave birth to a son who would become famous as Chief Bowles of the Western Cherokees.[9] Bowles had joined the class of white men who gave up their Anglo existence in exchange for power and influence among the Indians or for the fortunes which could be reaped by working as traders.

Meanwhile, Chalmers had packed up and left Pensacola for New York. Although his leave of absence was listed on the rolls as lasting a period of six months, there's no indication that he ever returned to his unit in West Florida. The reason he rushed to British headquarters was put forth quite clearly in a letter to Edward Winslow from his deputy at Pensacola, Hugh Mackay Gordon:

> There is a dispute concerning the Rank of Lt. Col's. Allen & Chalmers, it has been referred to General Campbell who will not settle but conceives Allen has the preference. You must know who has the preference & I am sure, altho' Allen's not on the spot, you will endeavor to have justice done him. Chalmers goes to New York, & I believe principally with a view to get the Rank, for fear those Corps should be thrown together. For my part I ought to have some knowledge and I must confess I have no doubt but Allen should be the eldest which I told General Campbell.[10]

The same month, Campbell sent Clinton a letter hoping that the commander in chief would approve of his plan to join the Pennsylvania and Maryland Loyalists.

Chalmers's tactic of running to the principal's office worked. On August 12, Clinton wrote Campbell, saying: "The incorporating Allen's and Chalmer's Corps, which you recommend, cannot possibly take Place, on account of the Injustice which would be thereby done to Lieut. Colo. Chalmers."[11]

Chalmers may have scored a victory but there's no record that he ever returned to Florida. Even as he struggled for the superior rank over the Pennsylvania Loyalist commandant, he obviously had more irons in the fire. In 1779, just before Spain officially declared war on England, Chalmers wrote to Lord Francis Rawdon, Clinton's adjutant general. Turning from his *idée fixe* about the Chesapeake Bay, Chalmers now saw fit to try to influence the British theater of war in West Florida:

> This Province appears necessary to Spain, who at least seems invariably attached to it.... I would most humbly suggest a wish that Great Britain in exchange for Port Rico would cede East & West Florida. Perhaps this would tend to create that natural alliance which time must produce.... The supposed cession would most happily influence & tend to retain the Southern Colonies in obedience and a few Years posession of Port Rico would evince it to be the second if not the first Sugar Island of Great Britain.[12]

If the British hadn't followed Chalmers's suggestions about the Eastern Shore of Maryland, they weren't going to lend an ear to his latest ideas on tactics. The commanders certainly didn't need any help from Chalmers. They were going lose British West Florida all on their own.

Meanwhile, at Pensacola, Campbell had created the United Corps of Pennsylvania and Maryland Loyalists with no official clearance to do so. What's more, these united companies weren't disbanded for more than a year. Campbell alleged that he never received Clinton's letter of August 12 telling him *not* to unite the two regiments. In Campbell's defense, keeping the units separate did seem a bit silly. As he noted in a letter to Clinton in May 1780, "Bringing them back to 10 or 11 Companies will make a monstrous Proportion of Commissioned and Non-Commissioned Officers to men."[13] Campbell's failure to receive the counterorder may have been his revenge against James Chalmers for going over his head straight to Sir Henry.

The Maryland Loyalists weren't on their best behavior. In December, Gordon was chagrined to tell Winslow in a letter that the men of the Provincial line had not been idle. With nothing to keep them occupied, they were fighting each other. Gordon noted that Captain Isaac Costen, Lieutenant James Miller, and Ensign Winder Cannon of the Maryland Loyalists had been brought before a general courtmartial for "cudgelling." Gordon was quick to note, however, that this fighting was only taking place in the Provincial line.[14]

The loyalists would soon have something more to do than fight among themselves. Commander Campbell had decided that the garrison fortress in the center of Pensacola was inadequate for the army's needs. One concern was that it wasn't large enough. A bigger concern was Gage Hill, about twelve hundred yards north of town. Campbell knew that if the Spanish ever got possession of the hill and rained cannon fire down upon them, the British would be unable to hold the town. He ordered construction on the southeast side of Gage Hill of a wooden stockade fort to be called Fort George. To protect the fort, he also ordered construction of a defense work on the northwest end of the hill, to be called the Queen's Redoubt. Work was begun as well on a Prince of Wales Redoubt situated between the Queen's Redoubt and Fort George. All of this construction was now the sole occupation of the soldiers in the garrison.

Campbell next decided to build fortifications at Red Cliffs, located at the entrance to Pensacola Bay. More than a dozen Maryland Loyalists helped navy seamen construct the works, which were soon dubbed the Royal Navy Redoubt. It was thought that a few pieces of heavy artillery perched on the cliffs would discourage a fleet of ships trying to force its way into the bay.

Across the entrance of the harbor from Red Cliffs was the western tip of Santa Rosa Island. Campbell believed that a battery here in addition to the one at Red Cliffs would make the bay impenetrable, and he ordered works to be built. Unfortunately, there weren't enough men or materials to support all of this construction at once. To the doom of the garrison at Pensacola, the defenses on Santa Rosa Island were never finished.

Not far to the west, Spanish Commander Bernardo de Galvez, who had been appointed governor of Louisiana in 1776, captured Mobile and fortified it against an attack from the British at Pensacola. Galvez guessed that the British simply couldn't pass up such a tempting target.

Attack on Mobile

By January 7, 1781, Campbell had grown restless waiting for the Spanish to attack him. He decided to attack Galvez's forces at Mobile instead. Without waiting for reinforcements, he sent out sixty men of the German Waldeck Regiment, one hundred men of the Sixtieth Regiment, four hundred Indians, and more than two hundred Pennsylvania and Maryland Provincials. At dawn, they attacked the Spanish post with bayonets. In the bitter hand-to-hand fighting, several officers fell dead, including Colonel Von Hanxleden of the Waldecks and Lieutenant James Gordon of the Sixtieth Regiment.

With so many officers killed, the command now fell to Captain Philip Barton Key. He was in a difficult position but made a calm and wise decision. The Waldecks had lost their leader and they couldn't speak English. Any attempt to further the attack would be disastrous if orders were misunderstood. Key "judged it prudent to order a retreat" and the expedition limped back to Pensacola.[15]

While the raid had been a failure, the conduct of officers like Key was noticed by Campbell. He noted they "did everything that zeal and honor could dictate for the success of His Majesty's arms."[16]

Among the hundreds of Indians who accompanied the British and Germans was William Augustus Bowles. His loyalist officer's coat gone, the seventeen-year-old was now clad in "savage" attire. Leading a group of Lower Creeks, Bowles wouldn't leave the battle. He continued to pour fire into the Spanish ranks. Only after a cannon ball shattered a tree that Bowles was using for cover did he quit the field.[17]

The always unpredictable Bowles shortly thereafter rejoined his old regiment at Pensacola after a lapse of nearly two years. Placed in Captain Frisby's company, he found himself sharing grim circumstances: There was going to be a siege, and the British and Provincial troops knew they had little chance of holding out for long without help.

The Siege

On March 9, 1781, the Spanish fleet arrived off Santa Rosa Island. Field Marshal Bernardo de Galvez wanted Pensacola and he had the manpower necessary to accomplish his goal. The two British ships in the area, *Mentor* and *Port Royal*, were forced to withdraw after the Spanish heavy artillery began firing on them. The Spanish invasion force was delighted to discover the works on Santa Rosa Island consisted of nothing more than three dismounted cannons and a partly demolished breastwork. And when the Royal Navy Redoubt at Red Cliffs opened up on the Spanish ships, the guns did little damage.

By the 24th, Galvez's troops had crossed Pensacola Bay under fire and begun looking for a place to land. On the 26th, they landed between Moore's Lagoon and Sutton's Lagoon. An attack by a large band of Indians slowed them down but inflicted little damage. They were closing in on the British defenses now. When they were close enough, they would dig in and bring their heavy artillery pieces into action.

As the Spanish forces cautiously moved across Sutton's Lagoon to get closer to Fort George, they ran into a detachment of Maryland Loyalists at one of the advance British posts. The Marylanders finally got their first taste of war. A journal noted:

> *Friday 30th.* About 8 o'clock an advanced picquet under the command of Captain [Patrick] Kennedy of the Maryland Loyalists was obligded to retreat as the enemy was marching down upon them and began to fire their field pieces[.] 10 o'clock Capt. Kenedys party marched down to Neils Meadows about a mile and a quarter from our works.... The Indians came in and brought with them 4 of the enemys drums, 1 head and a number of scalps.[18]

Galvez began the slow task of reconnoitering the hills northwest of Fort George and its redoubts, looking for the best placement of his heavy guns. It was officially a siege now.

The garrison sensed the slim chance they had of holding out, and some soldiers in the fort weren't interested in being caged. Like rats deserting the proverbial sinking ship, the first of the Maryland Loyalist deserters showed up in the Spanish camp on March 31. Galvez's battle diary noted:

> At 7 o'clock at night a deserter from the Maryland Regiment arrived with the news that General Campbell planned another attack like the one the previous afternoon and that in the town there were 600 equipped troops, 300 sailors, many armed Negroes, and a great number of Indians encamped under the protection of Fort George. [19]

Deserters from all the regiments soon found their way into the Spanish camp. On Saturday the 7th, an unusual incident occurred:

> A Lieutenant from the Maryland Regiment presented himself to the General [Galvez], asking to serve under his orders; for some time now he had left the English service due to a dispute which he had had with his Captain and was enroute to Georgia by foot when he learned of our arrival.
> Through this officer and several other deserters that arrived, the General learned that the Indians were retreating; that they busied themselves in robbing the houses of the inhabitants.... [20]

It seems impossible that the officer in question could have been anyone other than William Augustus Bowles. Bowles had resigned after an argument with a superior officer. That the former ensign would be mistaken for a lieutenant isn't very strange, as there was no visual distinction between the two ranks. Alternatively, it wouldn't have been out of character for Bowles to upgrade his old commission just because he felt like it. To add to the confusion, there is no record of exactly when Bowles rejoined the Maryland Loyalists. Unfortunately, Galvez didn't say what happened to this informer after their meeting. However, it would appear that Bowles, for reasons unknown, returned to the British lines shortly thereafter. He may have been looking to join up with whoever could give him the best offer, and he chose the British.

Years later, the U.S. Commissioner of Indian Affairs called William Augustus Bowles "an American of low, mean extraction." Loyalist historian Lorenzo Sabine branded him "a bold and wicked man."[21] If this heretofore unexamined incident is true and Bowles was willing to sell out his former comrades, the harsh accusations were perhaps understated.

On April 14, the Maryland Loyalists were again supplying the enemy with information: "At 4 o'clock in the afternoon a deserter from the Maryland Regiment arrived and after being questioned by the General stated among other things that on the afternoon of the 12th there had been several Indians wounded and one English officer killed."[22]

In the latter half of April, the pattern continued unchanged for the two sides. The Spanish extended their line of trenches to the northwest while the British, Provincials, and Indians periodically came out to halt or at least hinder their progress. They slowed the Spanish somewhat but the outcome wasn't going to change. The enemy was improving its position daily.

The siege was dotted with strange sights and horrible misfortunes. On May 3, the British, Germans, and Royal Provincials picked up nearly four hundred cannon balls that the Spanish had fired at them. Most of these were returned to the enemy, courtesy of the Royal Artillery pieces. Two days later, a seaman belonging to the *Port Royal* was picking up cannon balls when he was struck "in the britch" by a twenty-four-pound cannon ball. The britch of a musket referred to the butt of the gun, so the location of the unfortunate seaman's wound can easily be imagined. Needless to say, he died shortly afterward.[23]

On the following morning, the Queen's Redoubt was making it difficult for the Spanish to return fire. Galvez's journal noted: "All that

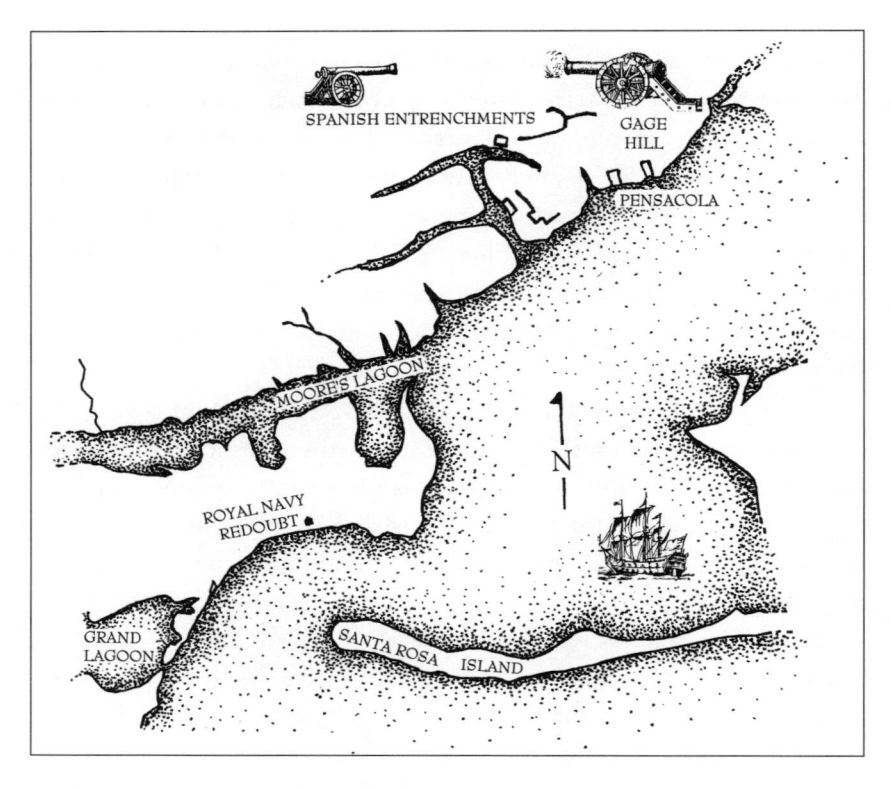

The siege of Pensacola, 1781. The British and Provincial forces never stood a chance against the superior Spanish forces (based on contemporary maps).

morning the enemy directed a continuous and fairly well-aimed firing at our position, but particularly at 1 o'clock they took it up with such vigor, firing grapeshots, bombs, and grenades...."[24]

What was happening, of course, was that the British artillery were softening up the Spanish in preparation for an assault. As they dropped for cover, the Spanish failed to notice a large detachment emerge from the Queen's Redoubt. Two hundred men advanced quickly and quietly on the Spanish works with bayonets fixed. In the lead were about one hundred Marylanders and Pennsylvanians under the command of Maryland Loyalist Major John MacDonald. Coming up to support them was the German Waldeck regiment under De Horn.[25]

Charging with bayonets had made the reputation of the British army. The rebel armies to the north had lived for years in absolute terror of facing British bayonet charges. The Royal Provincials quickly proved that they could match the regulars in ruthless efficiency. They caught the Spanish completely unprepared as they leapt into the redoubt. In terror, the Spanish fell back to the other redoubt but the attackers, their blood lust up, followed. Eighteen Spanish soldiers were killed by bayonet or by the sword of an officer. One Provincial sergeant, apparently of the Pennsylvania regiment, was killed. The attackers quickly returned to the first redoubt and spiked the Spanish cannons. Spiking a cannon entailed hammering an iron nail into the touchhole of the piece, rendering it useless until the nail could be removed. Leaving the trench on fire, they returned to their own lines.

The attack was but a brief moment where the Maryland Loyalists showed that, when given the opportunity, they could do the job as well as any British regulars. In spite of the hardship of the siege, desertions had actually dropped off to almost nothing in the Maryland unit. In the heat of battle, the loyal Marylanders were standing shoulder-to-shoulder with the British. Campbell wrote that he was "perfectly supported" by Major MacDonald and the Waldeck commander "in their attention to order, discipline and alertness on duty." Further, they "performed with a forward zeal and alacrity."[26] However, any satisfaction regarding the successful sortie was short-lived.

Tuesday, May 8, seemed like every other day since the siege began. It was going to be a long day of artillery pieces exchanging fire, Spanish troops digging trenches ever closer, and the defenders of Fort George hoping for a miracle. At 6 A.M., the British cannons in the Queen's Redoubt opened up against the Spanish, who returned fire with two howitzers. Around 9 A.M., a group of seamen and the Pennsylvania Loyalists were receiving their allotments of gunpowder from the magazine of the besieged redoubt. Suddenly, a shell came through the door of the magazine and detonated the kegs of powder. The explosion was enormous, leveling the fortification to a pile of rubble. Forty-five Pennsylvania Loyalists lay dead along with forty seamen.

A Spanish advance was repelled long enough for the wounded to be carried to safety. By ten o'clock, the enemy had possession of the remains of the redoubt and were soon firing on the Prince of Wales Redoubt. The artillery pieces pounded away at each other at close distance. Camp follower Elizabeth Woodward, the wife of Maryland Loyalist Private Samuel Woodward, later described how she used pieces of her clothing as wadding for the cannons in this furious encounter.[27]

Despite the efforts of the defenders, the battle was lost. The Crown forces could hold on only at the expense of countless lives. By midafternoon, a flag of truce was hoisted from the British lines. Campbell was asking for terms of surrender.

In the ensuing articles of capitulation, the British would be allowed to return to any British port they desired and the soldiers and sailors "will not serve against Spain or her allies until such time as an exchange is verified for an equal number of Spanish prisoners or those of her allies."[28] The Provincials were going home, provided they didn't return to Florida. It was a stipulation with which the Marylanders were only too happy to comply.

Two days later, the British, Germans, and Provincials marched out from their lines and surrendered their arms to the Spanish. They had been granted all the honors of war for the surrender. The soldiers marched out with their muskets shouldered, the drums were allowed to beat, and the vibrant colors of the king's standard flew in the breeze as the companies marched from their redoubts. Soon after, the soldiers boarded vessels which would take them to Havana before they were returned to New York.

Though the siege was lost, the commander had changed his mind about the loyalists he had dismissed as "Irish vagabonds." It would have been very easy for Campbell to say Pensacola was lost because he was burdened with too many inexperienced Provincials. That explanation would have been accepted, even encouraged, at headquarters. Instead, he wrote:

> Notwithstanding the mixture of corps, and the consequent incohesion and disunity of action that might have thence been apprehended, yet I have the pleasure to say, that the handful of troops, both officers and soldiers, under my command, seemed animated with vigor and spirit to the last, and eager to distinguish themselves; even the dispiriting circumstances of frequent desertions, appeared not to affect or discourage those who remained, but to excite to vengeance and resentment.[29]

For a British officer, this was a compliment of the highest order. Under almost impossible circumstances, the British and Royal Provincials had served with honor. Despite requests, they were never given proper reinforcements and stores of ordnance were never received.

Given the adversity, the loyalists proved that they too had a stiff upper lip. Had the Spanish failed, everyone at Fort George probably would have been mentioned in dispatches. Unfortunately, the rest of the world didn't much care one way or the other what was going on in Florida. Washington trapped Cornwallis five months later at Yorktown. *That* was the news story of the year.

RETURN TO NEW YORK

By the end of the summer of 1781, the Maryland Loyalists returned to their old haunts in Newtown on Long Island where they were about as useful to the British as the last time they had been there. They sat for months with little to do.

Captain Walter Dulany, soon to be Major Dulany, was sent into the city on recruiting service.[30] His efforts were fruitless. The war was

By 1782, the ranks were dwindling rapidly in size as shown by the muster roll from Daniel Dulany Addison's company which consists of only eight privates. Of these eight, two were still held prisoner by Spain. Courtesy Maryland Historical Society, Baltimore.

grinding to a halt in the political aftermath of Yorktown. With the hostile enemies of France and Spain at her door, England had stretched herself too thin. Quite simply, the British couldn't fight the entire world. Diplomatic negotiations would soon begin in Paris. The war would be over as soon as the two sides ironed out the wrinkles.

The Maryland muster rolls began to dwindle. Captain Key became ill and took a leave of absence in December of 1782.[31] He boarded a boat for England where he would remain for three years, trying to figure out how to get back to Maryland. In the spring of 1783, Captain Frisby resigned his commission, apparently for health reasons as well.

The months dragged on. Ensign Bowles, used to an adventurous life, found himself in charge of woodcutting details and other equally mundane tasks. He tried to raise his sinking spirits by joining in the theater productions of the British officers. At one point, echoing the Indian outfits he had worn just a short time before, Bowles appeared in Moorish costume as Zanga in Edward Young's *Revenge* at the John Street Theater.[32]

His performance in *Revenge* was loaded with irony: The character of Zanga hated the Spanish. In the years after the Revolution, Bowles would fight Spain with the same determination as his character. Like Major John André had done in Philadelphia, he painted some of the background scenery himself. Like André, Bowles was destined to die at an early age.

7

Exiles

At the same time that I acted with the greatest zeal against my rebellious countrymen, I never forgot that I was an American.

—Walter Dulany
Major, First Battalion of Maryland Loyalists

The Great Exodus

The war was finally coming to an end officially. New York City, the center of British operations since 1776, would soon be turned over to the Americans. The question was, "What will happen to the loyalists (military and civilians) when the bluecoats march in?" The answer at first was anything but clear.

Patriots like Alexander Hamilton and Patrick Henry, men at the forefront of the Revolution, now preached acceptance of the loyalists, or at least tolerance. When told that the loyalists were dangerous, Henry exclaimed, "Afraid of them?—what, sirs, shall *we* who have laid the proud British lion at our feet, now be afraid of his whelps?"[1]

A more important issue was at stake: the image of the new country. Hamilton received a letter on the subject from John Jay, statesman, diplomat, and future chief justice of the United States, who was in Paris working on the peace negotiations. Jay proclaimed:

> The Tories are almost as much pitied in these countries as they are execrated in ours; an undue degree of severity toward them would, therefore, be impolitic as it would be unjustifiable. They, who incline to involve that whole class of men in indiscriminate punishment and ruin, certainly carry the matter too far. It would be an instance of unnecessary rigour and unmanly revenge, without a parallel. . . . Victory and peace should in my mind be followed by clemency, moderation and benevolence, and we should be careful not to sully the glory of the revolution by licentiousness and cruelty.[2]

The common people weren't quite as willing to forgive and forget. Public image was something for politicians to worry about. For the average embittered citizen, personal vengeance was to be utilized whenever possible. To be sure, there was plenty to avenge: Tarleton's bloody raids in the Carolinas, the tory and Indian atrocities at Cherry Valley and all along the Mohawk Valley. The war wounds were going to take a long time to heal.

To the masses of loyalists trapped in New York City, it was easy to perceive that there was no going home. John Siger, a soldier of the Loyal American Regiment, thought he would leave the city and speak with some old friends. Once outside the city, he was seized by four men who beat him, shaved his head (a very nasty gesture in the eighteenth century), and threatened to chop his head off before sending him back "to let his friends on Long Island know that every rascal of them that attempted to come back among them would meet with the like accident."[3]

The loyal Marylanders were as hesitant to return home as the others. There was no reason to believe Maryland would be any more tolerant of them than other states. Although punishment was relatively light for loyalists who had stayed at home and kept their mouths shut, any Marylander who was known to have fought in a loyalist regiment knew his home had long since been confiscated. His old neighbors, even if they didn't kill him outright, would never give him a moment's peace. The ever-dwindling membership of the First Battalion of Maryland Loyalists prepared to leave with the enormous loyalist exodus, their destination: the Canadian frontier of Nova Scotia.

As they bided their time in New York waiting for transport, some Maryland Loyalist officers tried to put themselves on a better financial footing. On May 27, Lieutenant John Sterling sent a memorial to Commander in Chief Guy Carleton in which he reminded his superior that he had willingly accepted a lieutenant's commission rather than that of captain in 1777 when he was told he was young and inexperienced. Noting the recent resignation of Captain James Frisby, Sterling asked for his company. He hoped that a captain's commission would "render him independent of his infatuated Countrymen, who appear, too evidently, still to retain a peculiar bitterness and inveterate resentment against those who have fought in defence of their King and Constitution." His memorial contained a cover letter by Chalmers in which the lieutenant colonel praised his zeal and merit as an officer.[4] Carleton was convinced and Sterling left New York as a captain.

Dozens of ships sailed back and forth between New York and Nova Scotia in the summer and fall of 1783 transporting hordes of loyalists to their new homes. The loyalist newspaper *Rivington's Royal Gazette* was filled with announcements of the various arrivals and departures of ships involved in the mass migration. Page after page of advertisements showed the loyalists selling off all the things they knew they couldn't take with them.

Finally in early September, the Maryland Loyalists and their families boarded a ship bound for Saint John. Several officers, including Philip Barton Key and James Chalmers, had already left for London. Handouts of land in Canada weren't enough for them. They had lost a fortune when their properties were taken. Presenting their cases in person would increase their chances of a profitable settlement. Little did they suspect they would miss the regiment's final adventure.

The *Martha*

In the early morning hours of September 23, 1783, the transport ship *Martha* had made its way to Cape Sable, just off the southern tip of Nova Scotia. The other ships in the loyalist fleet had made better time and were already docked at Saint John. Packed below decks were the remnants of the companies of Patrick Kennedy, Daniel Dulany Addison, Caleb Jones, John Sterling, Levin Townsend, and Philip Barton Key, as well as part of DeLancey's Second Battalion from New York. Kennedy, who was now commanding officer of the Maryland Loyalists in Chalmers's absence, wound up describing the voyage of the *Martha* in his journal. He little suspected the ending would be so dramatic. Nearby, a pregnant Elizabeth Woodward held one of her children in her arms. Her services to king and country were already the stuff of legend. Now, she was going to add one more harrowing chapter to her life.

Having finally escaped the clutches of the rebels, the loyalists were probably hopeful for a chance to start over in the Canadian wilderness. But luck had seldom, if ever, been on the side of the First Battalion of Maryland Loyalists; this particular Tuesday morning would prove no different.

The master of the ship, Captain Willis, had left the port of New York with a complement of old sails. Rather than replace the rotting canvas, he decided for reasons known only to him to risk it. It was a decision he would live to regret. The aging sails may have weathered the long journey without a problem—if the ship hadn't run into a bad storm.

On deck, things weren't going well for the *Martha*. The transport ship was rocked back and forth by the waves. A skeleton crew of twelve, composed of seamen and mere boys, struggled for a number of hours to rig and set up a new main topsail to replace the one which had been ripped to shreds by high winds earlier in the evening. Their minds on the task at hand, no one apparently noticed how close to the shore they were being pushed by the currents.

At 4 A.M., the ship struck a ledge of rocks between Cape Sable and the Seal Islands. The soldiers of the two regiments tried desperately to keep the pumps clear. Seeing that they were fighting a losing battle, they asked the captain to get the lifeboats out, but he refused, believing that the ship would work itself free. In the hold, the water level rose rapidly. Seeing at last that it was hopeless, Willis ordered the boats out. These consisted of a cutter, a longboat, and a jolly boat (similar to a dinghy). Unfortunately, as soon as the longboat was in the water, the *Martha*'s mainmast suddenly fell on it, smashing it to pieces.

Many on board must have realized then that their chances of survival had nearly vanished. They had long since lost contact with the other ships of the loyalist fleet, and by now the ship was full of water but fast aground on the rocks. The waves crashed over the deck, soaking the unlucky soldiers and their families. The ship was intact for now, but at any moment they could be tossed into cold, hostile waters and left to drift for days or perhaps weeks.

The captain ordered the jolly boat over the side and "to the surprise of every body—after repeatedly proclaiming that he would be one of the last to leave the ship, he jumped into her as she went over the side, rowed to the cutter, which lay off, [and] got into her," declared Patrick Kennedy in later testimony.[5] In desperation, several seamen and six soldiers, two of them Maryland Loyalists, swam out to the cutter and climbed on board.

A panicked Willis moved the little boat away from the wreck, leaving the jolly boat adrift in the churning waters. The unlucky passengers could only watch as their means of escape drifted away into the darkness, completely empty. The loyalists called out to the captain, demanding that he "come towards the stern of the ship and concert some plan for the General safety and to comfort the poor Unhappy Souls on Board."[6] Their cries were in vain. Like the jolly boat, the captain's little craft disappeared from sight.

Within a short time, the ship went to pieces. Men, women, and children attached themselves to parts of the wreck. Lieutenants James

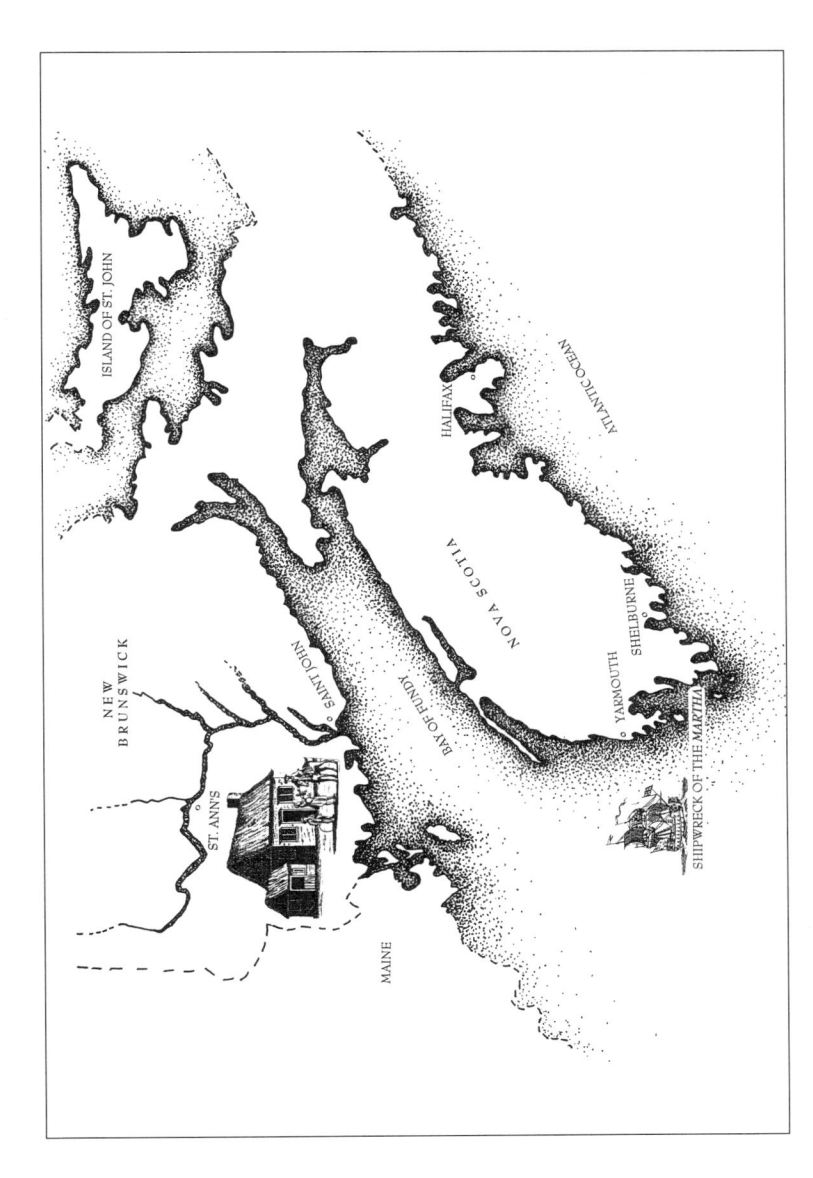

The exiled Maryland Loyalists found themselves in St. Ann's (Fredericton) in 1784. Most arrived with nothing, their possessions having been lost in the shipwreck of the *Martha*.

Henley and William Sterling and surgeon William Stafford shared a piece of wreckage. To their great dismay, they floated at sea for two days and two nights, the freezing water nearly to their waists. Young William Sterling couldn't hold out any longer and perished. Their strength nearly at an end, Lieutenant Henley and Dr. Stafford drifted to an island on the third day. Their plight, however, was far from over. The island offered no possibility of food and they had no way of making a fire. Poorly clothed, they were marooned for seven days before being spotted.[7]

Other survivors were luckier, although not by much. After drifting in the open bay for thirty hours, four fishing boats appeared and collected the weary passengers. Samuel and Elizabeth Woodward were among those saved, Elizabeth still clutching her youngest child in her arms. Upon landing on shore, two of her sons were found among the small group of survivors. Her joy was turned to sorrow upon discovering a third son was dead.[8]

The speed of their rescue was not helped by the master of the *Martha*. According to the testimony of Lieutenant Henley, Dr. Stafford, and Lieutenant Michael Laffen of DeLancey's Battalion, Willis landed at the nearest settlement and stated that he believed everyone on board had died. To make matters worse, he "rather inclined to discourage their intentions of going to look out for the Wreck to save any person who might have survived than to push them forward to so charitable a deed or to offer his assistance to effect so good a purpose."[9]

Fortunately for the *Martha* passengers adrift in the bay, inhabitants of nearby Yarmouth and French settlers along the lower part of the coast descended on the location of the wreck. They were determined to locate any survivors. They were also determined to salvage anything they could from the wreck before anyone else had the opportunity. Kennedy noted with disgust that the salvagers took up cables, anchors, and other items of considerable value while the Maryland and New York loyalists had lost everything due to Willis's negligence.

Fifty-seven Marylanders are believed to have died when the *Martha* went down: one lieutenant, one ensign, six sergeants, two corporals, twenty-seven privates, seven women, nine children, and four servants. Of DeLancey's Second Battalion, fifty-eight drowned. For the approximately forty-five Marylanders still alive, surviving the sinking was only half the battle. They arrived in Saint John in a sorry state. Patrick Kennedy gave a statement to the *Nova-Scotia Gazette* in which he stated:

> We are here in a truly pitiable situation, having lost everything we had in the world; Major Prevost has, indeed, exerted every endeavour for our comfort and accomodation, and has purchased blankets to cover the men; but the loss of our ammunition, arms, and accoutrements, with that of our stores, bedding, and utensils, is very severely felt, as we are anxious to get up the River to our Lands.[10]

The lands were now all they had. For the loyal Marylanders, the final destination lay miles upriver from the port of Saint John. At the tiny town of St. Ann's, land was available for several loyalist regiments. For now, though, they were stranded at Saint John.

"Nothing but Wilderness"

Nova Scotia was a distinct culture shock to most of the three thousand loyalists in the fall of 1783. They hadn't realized until now how relatively easy life in the colonies had been. Forced out of the bustling city of New York, they had been packed off to what must have seemed like the most remote corner of the world. To the Maryland Loyalists, this was Pensacola all over again, only now they would simply freeze to death rather than drop dead from tropical diseases. The endless forests were similar to those that had greeted the first North American settlers in the early 1600s. There was one important difference, though: This land, unlike

Virginia or Maryland, was much colder and much harsher—unforgiving to anyone who couldn't acclimate quickly enough. The patriots called this place "Nova Scarcity" with good reason.

One loyalist woman climbed to the top of a hill and later recounted: "I watched the sails disappearing in the distance, and such a feeling of loneliness came over me that, although I had not shed a tear through all the war, I sat down on the damp moss with my baby in my lap and cried."[11] Others were just as disappointed. One loyalist on the other side of the bay in Shelburne (not far from where the *Martha* foundered) noted with anger:

> All our golden promises are vanished in smoke. We were taught to believe that this place was not barren and foggy, as had been represented, but we find it ten times worse. We have nothing but his Majesty's rotten pork and unbaked flour to subsist on. . . . It is the most inhospitable 'clime that ever mortal set foot on.[12]

The sudden influx of so many people created temporary havoc. A shortage of boats kept the exiles from getting up the river to their land. Some were living in log houses and huts; a large number were living in tents. As winter set in, the families still in tents tried to thatch their canvas homes with spruce boughs to keep out the cold. Despite their best efforts, a number of women and children died during the winter from exposure and a lack of food. The Maryland loyalists, with nothing but the clothes on their backs and a few blankets, were apparently left to fend mostly for themselves.

A Shaky Start

It was now the job of the eclectic collection of loyalists to change Nova Scotia from a nearly uninhabited wilderness into a prosperous colony. Just how that was going to be done and who was going to reap the benefits was still a matter of debate. Behind the scenes, a feud had already started brewing among the loyalists.

In July of 1783, before most of the refugees even landed at Saint John and Halifax, a group of wealthy and influential loyalists (including Ward Chipman, the deputy muster master general of the Provincial forces) sent a petition to Commander in Chief Guy Carleton at New York. They wanted land, lots of it. Each of the fifty-five men was asking for five thousand acres of land for the very basic reason that they had been wealthy and influential in the colonies before the war. Using phrases like "Considering our several Characters, and our former Situations in Life," they felt it natural enough that they should be the financial magnates in the colony of exiled loyalists. They also attached a hint of warning saying that, by giving them all the power (and a big chunk of the land), it "will be highly Advantageous in diffusing and supporting a Spirit of Attachment to the British Constitution as well as To His Majesty's Royal Person and Family."[13] It was an interesting idea—the hoi polloi wouldn't stay loyal unless a few well-chosen, well-paid loyalists were there to remind them to live their lives for king and country.

The loyalists had already lost everything once and they weren't prepared to let it happen again. A petition containing more than six hundred loyalist signatures soon reached Carleton.

> That chagrined as your Memorialists [the loyalists] are at the manner in which the late Contest has been terminated and disappointed as they find themselves in being left to the lenity of their Enemys on the dubious recommendation of their Leaders they yet hoped to find an Assylum under British Protection little suspecting there could be found amongst their Fellow suffers Persons ungenerous enough to attempt ingrossing to themselves so disproportionate a Share of what Government has alloted for their common benefit—and so different from the original proposals.[14]

The six hundred wanted to go forward; the wealthy fifty-five wanted to go back. To the fifty-five original petitioners, the older, familiar system of landlords and tenants worked just fine. But many tenants wanted no part of it; they weren't interested in being dependent on a newly created landed gentry. In some cases, the new landlords were the officers they had served under during the war—hardly a comforting prospect for those soldiers who hated their commanders.

The whole situation was a recipe for disaster. A few angry letters in the newspapers, well-timed public protests, and threats of violence could have erupted and thrown the new colony into revolt. It didn't happen, and the reasons were as simple as the difference between whigs and tories. Saint John wasn't Boston, and the loyalists weren't rebels. They would approach social change in the same way they had attempted it in the colonies before the war. Here, far away from the interference of their revolutionary neighbors, they quietly accomplished their goal.

It was a milieu in many ways unique to the new province. Major Edward Fitzgerald of the Fifty-fourth Regiment, upon observation of the social order of the refugees, later noted:

> The equality of everybody and of their manner of life I like very much. There are no gentlemen; everybody is on a footing (provided he works) and wants nothing; every man is exactly what he can make himself, or is made by industry. The more uneasiness about providing for them; as this is done by the profit of their work. By the time they are fit to settle, he can always afford them two oxen, a cow, a gun and an axe, and in a few years, if they work, they will thrive.[15]

Author Esther Clark Wright concluded in *The Loyalists of New Brunswick* that "the belief in constitutional procedure for redress of grievances, like the loyalty to the British crown one of the fundamental tenets of the Loyalists, meant patience and a conviction of the ultimate triumph of justice. It meant respect for law and order and for orderly procedure. It meant unwillingness to resort to violence, and willingness to wait for years rather than to jeopardize ultimate victory by depending on summary methods."[16]

This, of course, didn't mean that everyone would be pleased with some of the results. Edward Winslow, the muster master general of Royal Provincial forces who could trace his roots in America back to the *Mayflower*, disapproved of the careless granting of lands to any loyalist who had his hand out. "A great proportion of the original patentees were idle, dissipated, and capricious" and worse: "as soon as they were fairly in possession of their lands and had expended the bounty of government, they sold it for a trifle." Probably what Winslow couldn't stomach was the restructuring of society without his permission. "Our gentlemen have all become potato farmers and our shoemakers are preparing to legislate," he later observed unpleasantly.[17]

The Maryland Legacy

In the midst of this social restructuring, the Maryland Loyalists were nearly invisible. No one had suffered as much hardship as Chalmers's regiment. They made their way to St. Ann's, glad just to be alive. It wasn't a time for idle landowners watching from the porch as the tenants labored in his fields. In this rough land, everyone would have to get their hands dirty. Some would get their hands dirtier than others.

Patrick Kennedy and the dwindling band of Marylanders still under his command were issued their grant of 13,750 acres on July 14, 1784. Known as "Block 1," the land lay directly west across the Saint John River from the township of St. Ann's.

Their luck in the new land initially was about as good as their luck had been in the British Army. Winslow noted in a letter to his deputy commissary, "I am sorry for your friends of Block No. 1 who have scarcely a ration left among them."[18] Somehow, they made it through their first winter.

Still, some were not content with England's handout. By the end of 1784, twenty-three of the forty-eight Maryland Loyalist grantees had sold their lands. Some were simply not interested in farming. Others, perhaps hard up for cash, sold their lots to one of their enterprising captains, Caleb Jones, and continued to live on the land as tenants.[19] Their lives on Block 1 were quiet, with one notable exception. In 1785, George Smith, a ninety-two-year-old settler, complained that two of the Maryland Loyalists had dragged him out of his house for reasons unknown.[20]

Captain Patrick Kennedy, the senior officer of the Maryland Loyalists, was an avid supporter of the move to create a new province in 1784. In a letter to Winslow, he declared:

> We are convinced that there is no Person of any consideration or consequence on the River St. John ... who is not perfectly satisfied of the absolute necessity of forming a new Government on the other Side of the Bay of Fundy, as the very existence of the Settlements there depends upon it.[21]

Indeed, they were. Kennedy's comments came only a few weeks before the Maryland Loyalists received their land allotments, the first in the newly created province of New Brunswick. However, the new frontier apparently didn't satisfy Kennedy. He eventually boarded a boat and returned to his native Ireland where he lived out the rest of his days.[22] For a few, the sacrifices to king and country would continue. Elizabeth Woodward was eventually remarried, to Jeremiah Hopkins, a sergeant of the 104th (New Brunswick) Regiment of Foot. After the War of 1812, she petitioned the British government for a pension in consequence of her numerous services to England. Her losses were many as well:

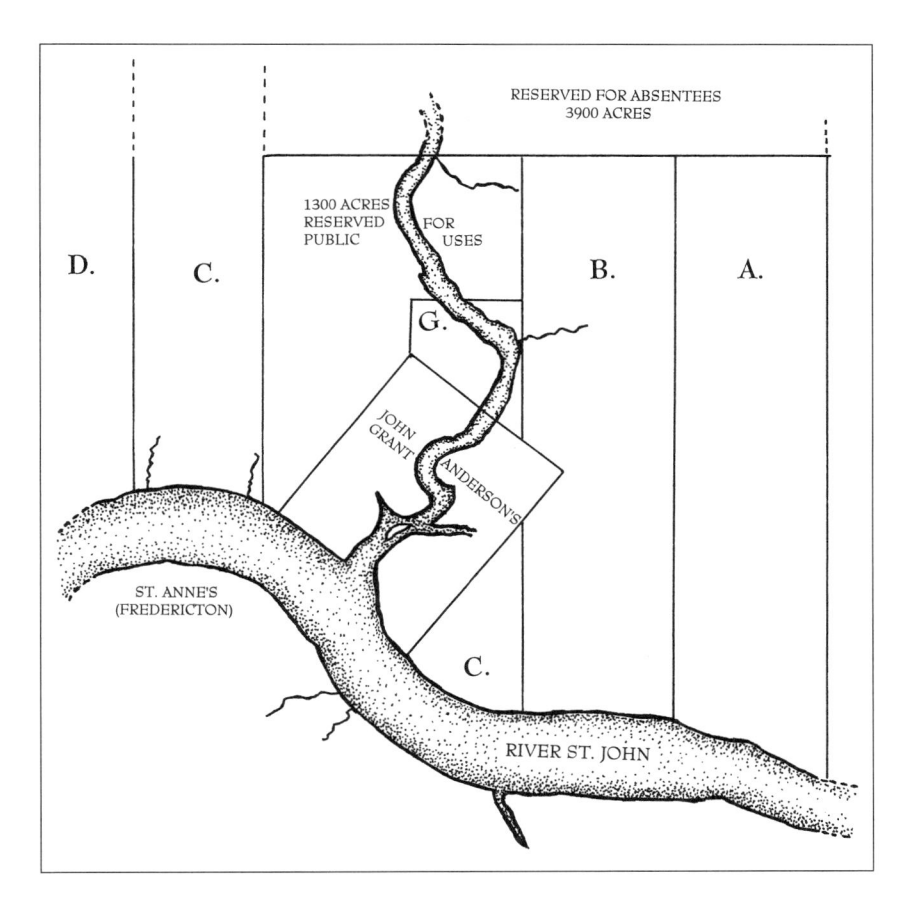

After a devastating shipwreck, the few remaining Maryland Loyalists received their land grant known as "Block 1" (based on microfilm #F16300, Kennedy Grant Plan, Maryland Loyalists, N.B. Archives).

At Sackett's Harbour, the pride of her heart, her twins fell; also [James] McDonough, her son-in-law. On hearing the news, she called her children 'round her, made them an animated speech, charged them to be revenged on the Yankees for their loss; and next time they went into action, they were cheered and encouraged by Mammy Hopkins, the name she went by in the regiment.[23]

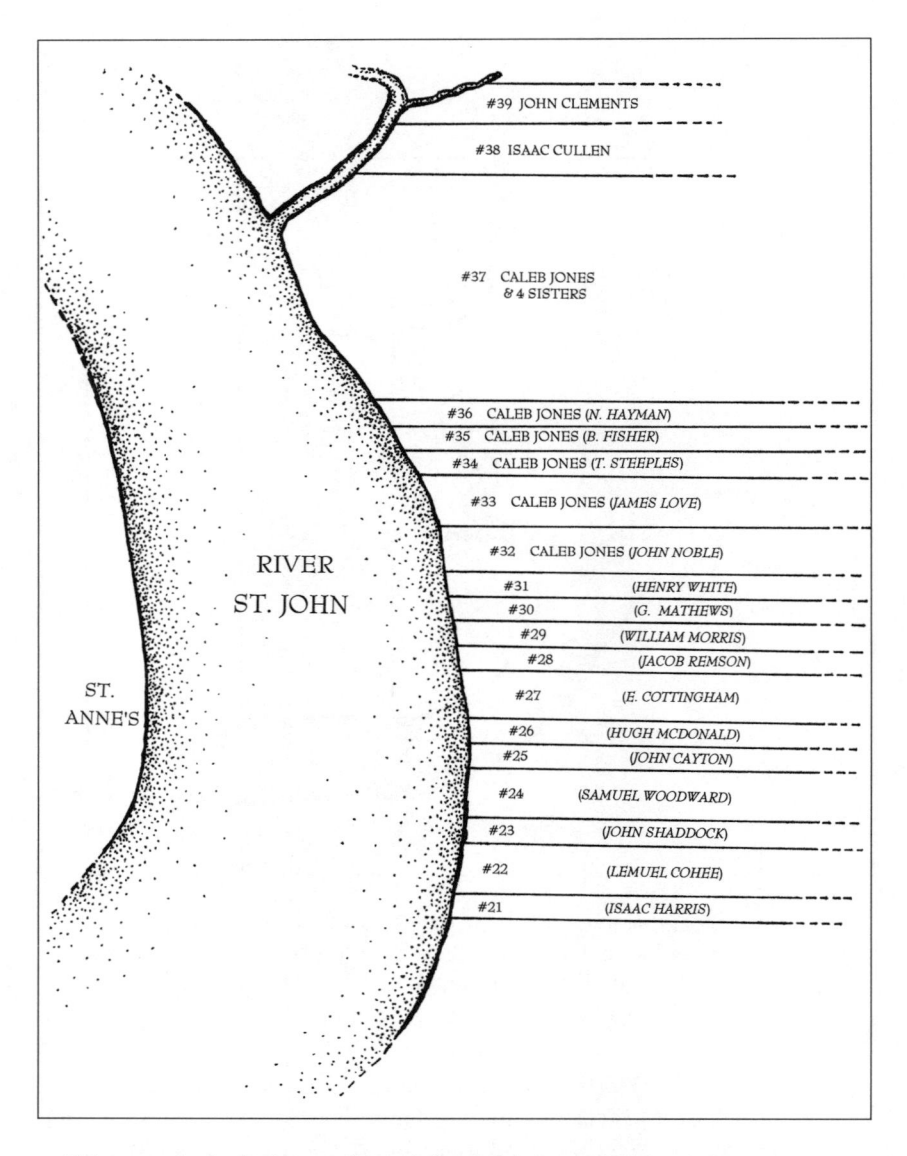

```
                            #39  JOHN CLEMENTS

                            #38  ISAAC CULLEN


                            #37  CALEB JONES
                                 & 4 SISTERS



                            #36  CALEB JONES (N. HAYMAN)
                            #35  CALEB JONES (B. FISHER)
                            #34  CALEB JONES (T. STEEPLES)

                            #33  CALEB JONES (JAMES LOVE)

               RIVER        #32  CALEB JONES (JOHN NOBLE)
              ST. JOHN      #31       (HENRY WHITE)
                            #30       (G. MATHEWS)
                            #29       (WILLIAM MORRIS)
   ST.                      #28       (JACOB REMSON)
  ANNE'S
                            #27       (E. COTTINGHAM)

                            #26       (HUGH MCDONALD)
                            #25       (JOHN CAYTON)

                            #24       (SAMUEL WOODWARD)

                            #23       (JOHN SHADDOCK)

                            #22       (LEMUEL COHEE)

                            #21       (ISAAC HARRIS)
```

Whatever he lacked in spelling skills, Caleb Jones had a gift for obtaining real estate. By 1788, he had added several Maryland loyalist properties to his own rather large grant (based on Map #6, St. John River from Mill Creek to Philles Creek, Frederickton Parish, York Co., RS 656/17-0, N.B, Archives). The italic print indicates Maryland loyalists who had sold their land grants by 1788.

And the Rest . . .

Some of the loyalist Marylanders never made it to New Brunswick. A few received permission while in New York to return to Maryland and did so unnoticed. Others went to regions unknown to start over.

As early as May 1782, James Chalmers's wife sought permission to leave Maryland to visit her husband in Elizabeth Town.[24] The purpose of the visit wasn't stated in her application but the uncertain status of Chalmers's lands in Maryland was undoubtedly on the lieutenant colonel's mind. He was destined to bicker with the state for the rest of his life about the family's Maryland property.

A few members of the regiment came to question their own loyalty and their ability to fight their neighbors. Major Walter Dulany wrote a letter to Guy Carleton on March 29, 1783, in which he acknowledged his appreciation to England. There was, however, a problem:

> My duty as a subject; the happiness which America enjoyed under the British Government; and the miseries to which she would be reduced by an independence; were the motives that induced me to join the British Army. . . . But, at the same time, that I acted, with the greatest zeal against my rebellious countrymen, I never forgot that I was an American. If, therefore, Sir, Independence should be granted, and the war still continued, I should deem it extremely improper to remain in a Situation obliging me to act either directly or indirectly against America. If, after this declaration, I can be received by your Excellency, upon the footing offered me by Colonel Thompson, I shall think myself highly honored, it being the first wish of my heart ever to serve in the British Army, whilst I can with consistency.[25]

Walter Dulany's desire to have it both ways didn't sit well with the British. Frederick Mackenzie, the deputy adjutant general, made a note on April 11 which contained Carleton's reaction to the letter: "If Independence is granted and the war continued, he [Dulany] cannot serve directly or indirectly against America. The King can have no occasion for the service of such officers, as will not serve against his enemies."[26]

So Dulany returned to his native Maryland, settled in Bladensburg, and married the widow of one Lloyd Dulany. (This Dulany, also a loyalist, had been killed in a duel in Hyde Park, London, in 1782. His opponent, Reverend Bennet Allen, had published an unfavorable comment in a London newspaper regarding Lloyd Dulany and other Americans with whom he was not pleased.[27]) Unhappy with conditions in Bladensburg, certain that any action they took would be undermined until there had been sufficient "time for the prejudices of the people against them to wear off," Dulany soon moved to Delaware.[28]

Even Maryland's last proprietary governor, Robert Eden, managed to return to his old home, Annapolis, after the war. Illness, however, took his life in September 1784. Today, his grave rests in the heart of the capital where he governed during Maryland's last days as an English colony.

8

Strange Days

We still have friends and warriors sufficient to stain your land with blood.
—William Augustus Bowles, 1791
(speaking to the U.S. Government)

No one could have predicted just how peculiar the fates of some Maryland loyalists would be.

WILLIAM AUGUSTUS BOWLES

The young Bowles found no comfort in accepting land in Nova Scotia, and when the *Martha* left New York harbor in early September on its ill-fated voyage to Saint John, the Maryland ensign was not aboard. Bowles wasn't destined to live out his days as an anonymous farmer in Canada—fate had a much more flamboyant end in store.

Tragically for Bowles, the evacuation meant a major threat to his lifestyle. When Washington's troops marched in to reoccupy the city, they would be busy cleaning up the mess the Crown forces had made since 1776. They weren't going to be interested in a troupe of foppish British and loyalist officers putting on the latest plays. Dennis Ryan's theatrical company broke up and Bowles followed several members of the company to the Bahamas.[1]

Resurfacing in Nassau, Bowles stayed around for a few years, passing his time in the town with other uprooted loyalists, acting in plays and painting the occasional picture.[2] He was frequently in the company of John Murray, Earl of Dunmore, whose position as royal governor of Virginia had been cut short by the Revolution. Along with other former loyalists desperate for cash, Bowles became involved in smuggling operations between the Bahamas and Florida. Now dressed as part Indian, part British officer, he revived his military skills by drilling a company of men involved in the covert operations.

Eventually, he returned to the Florida territory where he resumed the friendships he had cultivated while serving at Pensacola. He soon began spying on Georgia legislators on behalf of the Creek Indians in an effort to discover what plans were afoot to interfere with Indian territory.

From this time on, he took to wearing his Indian garb on a regular basis. During a visit to London in 1791, the English painter Thomas Hardy (no relation to the famous author) portrayed him as an Indian chief wearing a cloth turban with an ostrich feather and red plumes, a half-moon silver gorget (perhaps the same neckpiece he had worn as a Maryland Loyalist officer), and trademark silver armbands over a white man's ruffled shirt (the shirt being one he'd worn as a Provincial officer).

Bowles had chosen to ally himself with a powerful group of Indians: The war had helped bring about the death of the Iroquois Six Nations in the north, and the Creeks were now the largest and best-organized Indian tribe anywhere east of the Mississippi River.

He would lead a colorful life, highlighted by a degree of fame, intrigue, and treachery. After an escape from Spanish incarceration, he visited London a number of times dressed in his exotic native clothing, creating quite a stir in the newspapers. Osborne's Hotel became his base of operations as he rekindled his friendship with Benjamin Baynton, the former Pennsylvania Loyalist lieutenant with whom he had served at Pensacola. Baynton published an account of Bowles's life for an eager

Resplendent in his Creek Indian attire, William Augustus Bowles
sat for this portrait by British artist Thomas Hardy in 1791. It is the only
known painting of a Maryland Loyalist officer. Courtesy the National Trust

London audience in a 1791 work entitled *The Authentic Memoirs of William Augustus Bowles, Esquire, Ambassador from the United Nations of Creeks and Cherokees, to the Court of London*. Bowles's portrait, painted in 1791, was also on public display. There was something in the spectacle of a handsome, well-spoken young white man parading about town in full Indian attire that created a seductive air of mystery.

Treated with all the attention given a visiting dignitary, Bowles's influence rose, and this position of power wasn't lost on the new American government. When a 1790 treaty with the Creeks was being arranged, President Washington and Secretary of War Henry Knox were disturbed by Bowles's influence, uncertain if he was acting as some kind of liaison between the Creeks and the English government. This, of course, is exactly what he *was* doing. Maybe it wasn't official but that certainly didn't matter to Bowles.

The Maryland native had powerful Canadian contacts as well. John Graves Simcoe, formerly colonel of the Queen's Rangers, was now the lieutenant-governor of upper Canada. How well he could have remembered the youthful Bowles from Philadelphia or Long Island is a matter of debate. When Simcoe was ready to leave England for his new position, he received a letter from "that Active Adventurer, Bowles: he had served when a boy under my command. . . . To my surprise he talks of visiting me in Upper Canada."[3]

The U. S. government tried to come up with a plan to stem Bowles's growing influence with the Indians. At one point, they contemplated arresting his brother John, in hopes of curbing the director general's ambitions. John, who had recently returned to Maryland, hadn't committed any acts that could be considered treasonous, so the plan was dropped by President Washington. More anxiety, though, awaited the United States where Bowles was concerned.

Some two hundred miles east of Pensacola, Florida, lay the Spanish fort of St. Mark's. In April 1800, Bowles attacked it with his Indian allies. The attempt to overpower the fort should not have succeeded. In the past, Indians had always failed to maintain a prolonged assault against the white man's fortifications. This time, however, they were led by a white man who had been on the losing side of a prolonged siege. Since he had no artillery, Bowles knew the only effective course of action was to starve the Spaniards out, and it worked. On May 19, the fort surrendered to Bowles and his followers.

On hearing the news, President Thomas Jefferson reportedly declared that, if necessary, the United States would have to remove Bowles from St. Mark's.[4] Such actions, however, weren't necessary. Spanish ships soon arrived and pounded the walls of the fort to dust. Bowles and his Indian allies packed up and slipped quietly away.

William Augustus Bowles had made too many enemies to remain at liberty forever. President Jefferson and his secretary of war, Henry Dearborn, had debated how to get rid of him. The difficulty was that he wasn't a U.S. citizen, nor had he directly violated any U.S. laws. They could arrest him but a conviction might be impossible. Spain, however, had the goods on Bowles. He had already escaped from their custody once and was guilty of numerous offenses against the empire of Spain. If Bowles ever fell again into Spanish hands, they would have no trouble keeping him behind bars forever.

As the new century began, Bowles's power was declining. Powerful white men were gaining influence with the southeastern Indians. The end came in May 1803 when an Indian council was held at a sacred meeting place called Hickory Ground near present-day Montgomery, Alabama. White negotiators were anxious to convince the Upper and Lower Creeks, Seminoles, Cherokees, Chickasaws, and Choctaws to approve an extension of the Georgia boundary into their lands. The capture of William Augustus Bowles was also brought up. A large reward for Bowles was sure to leave him no place to hide.

Taking a very large risk, Bowles showed up at the council. It was to be a last-ditch effort to turn the Indians against Spain and the United States. If anyone could do that, it would be Bowles. Unfortunately, his luck had run out. He was captured and, a month later, found himself a guest of the Spanish, who locked him away in a cell at Havana's Morro

Castle. On December 23, 1803, Bowles died from starvation in the military hospital.[5] Whether this condition was entirely self-inflicted or imposed upon him was never discovered.

As the southeastern Indians were gradually swept away by the progress of white settlements, Bowles's legacy was soon a mere footnote. Had he lived longer, history books might have taken more notice of him. The War of 1812 may have turned out a bit differently if Bowles had united Indians in the south and acted in unison with Tecumseh's western Indians against the United States.

None of the former Maryland loyalists led a life quite as daring or full of adventure as Bowles. Certainly none represented such a direct threat to the United States as the young man from Frederick. Some even came home.

Philip Barton Key

To Philip Barton Key,
Who departed this life July 18, 1815

If nature's richest gifts could ever,
If genius, wit and eloquence, could charm,
If grief of sorrowing friends, or anguish wild
That wrings the widow's and the orphan's heart,
Could soothe stern death, and stay th' uplifted stroke,
Long had this victim of his wrath been spared.
Mourning survivors! let all care give place
To that great care that most demands your thoughts;
The care that brings the troubled soul to Christ;
Fix there your hopes. There is, beyond the grave,
A life of bliss, where death shall never more
Part you from joys that know no bound nor end.[6]

This rather unspectacular eulogy was written by Philip's nephew, Francis Scott Key, less than a year after the young lawyer had written "The Defence of Fort McHenry" during England's attempted capture of

Baltimore. Fortunately for Francis (and the country), the latter (soon to be known as "The Star-Spangled Banner") was far more inspired than the former.

In contrast to William Augustus Bowles, Captain Philip Barton Key was to establish himself as one of the United States' most industrious and patriotic citizens. When he presented a claim to the British government on June 21, 1785, he *seemed* just another dedicated loyalist. In his memorial, he is emphatic that he wasn't prompted to take different sides from his brother, a "firm Rebel." That he mentioned this at all seems to point up the fact that this sort of thing happened during the Revolution more often than some have thought. As his life would show, he may well have been the epitome of this cunning strategy.

Returning from England a short time later, Philip Barton found his lands had been confiscated by the state of Maryland. So brother John Ross Key divided his own lands and supported his brother until he was on his feet again. That didn't take very long.

While most former loyalists came back to their old residences to live a hopefully quiet existence, Philip Barton's nature could never have allowed such a thing. After practicing law for a time in Leonardtown, he moved north to the state capital of Annapolis where he quickly earned great respect as a lawyer and, consequently, captured a seat in the legislature as a Federalist.

Francis Scott Key, upon graduating from St. John's College in Annapolis, was eager to study in his native Frederick. Uncle Philip, however, made him realize that a real career as a lawyer required his presence in a large town such as Annapolis. Francis agreed and was soon in the state capital studying in the office of Judge Jeremiah Townley Chase and living under his uncle's roof.

As the 1790s progressed, Philip Barton Key's reputation grew, and Francis was always at his side, learning the profession. Philip's influence upon his nephew was enormous. From Uncle Philip, Francis learned an appreciation of English distractions such as fox hunting, which the former loyalist held dear.

Eventually Philip began to feel confined by Annapolis, and his ambitions soon led him to the new capital of the nation, Washington.

He had timed his move well. When Washington was little more than a tiny dismal town situated in a marsh, Philip moved in and established himself as the first lawyer of importance to reside close to the capitol. Kept busy as an attorney for the commissioners of the city, he quickly took Francis Scott on as a partner.[7] Soon, they were making a fortune.

In 1804, Philip and his nephew helped represent aging Supreme Court Justice Samuel Chase, a signer of the Declaration of Independence, in impeachment hearings. On opposite sides during the war, Chase and Key were both Federalists now, though how well the two knew each other is uncertain. Philip, however, was so busy that he had little time to devote to the case. He had bigger plans for his ambition: the U.S. Congress.

Key retired from his law practice and handed the office over to Francis. He ran for Congress as a Federalist which, of course, meant finding as much wrong as possible with Thomas Jefferson's administration. In the elections of 1806, Philip Barton Key found himself in the House of Representatives. Apparently the voters didn't have a problem with voting for a former loyalist officer in the British army: When his election was contested, Key responded, "I returned to my country like a prodigal [son] to his father, felt as an American should feel, was received and forgiven, of which the most convincing proof is my election."[8]

His time in Congress was respectable, if unspectacular. His success in private life had exceeded that of his fellow congressmen and enabled him to have the distinction of being the only member of either house of Congress who owned his own house in the town of Washington.[9] When war loomed in 1812 and Congress voted on whether to go to war with Great Britain, Philip Barton predictably voted against such action. As history would show, the measure passed.

At his mansion, called Woodley, Philip entertained the likes of Chief Justice John Marshall (an officer in the Virginia Continental Line during the Revolution and now a Federalist) and John Randolph (an understudy of ardent whig Patrick Henry).[10] He was elected to two terms before dying in the summer of 1815, shortly after the conclusion of the War of 1812. The *Federal Gazette* was quite kind about the old tory:

> In the trying period which preceded and followed the declaration of the late war he was a member of Congress, where his masterly exertions were never wanting to avoid the needless provocations to hostility, to preserve our commerce and peace, and for the re-establishment of that blessing as soon as it could be regained.[11]

It was a glowing tribute to the most successful loyalist from any colony who had returned to the United States. Only winning the presidency could have topped that, and Philip Barton Key probably pondered that possibility as well.

Robert Alexander

After the Revolutionary War, there was no way Robert Alexander was ever going to be allowed to return to his property at the Head of Elk. (The former Continental Congressman's valuable Elkton holdings comprised most of the land upon which the present town is built.) The state council of Maryland had no intention of being lenient with such a high-profile loyalist living under British protection.

Alexander was the closest thing Marylanders had to a Benedict Arnold. He had been at the seat of colonial power in 1775, privy to its secrets and knowledgeable about the inner workings of what would be the new government. When he joined the British army, he rendered every conceivable assistance to the enemy. His influence helped unite tories who worked to interfere with the patriots' war effort. There would be no homecoming for him.

From August 1782 to June 1783, the state sold off Alexander's possessions (land, slaves, books, etc.) for a total of six thousand three hundred pounds—a large amount, considering everything was sold at a fraction of its actual value.[12] Had the advertisements for Alexander's property appeared now, they would have been along the tawdry lines of: "A major East Coast tory has closed his doors forever. His loss is your gain! We'll practically be giving his land away! Don't pay too much!" Apparently, nobody did.

After Yorktown, from 1782 to September 1783, Alexander served on the British board which oversaw all money allowances to displaced loyalists. It was an important task. Unfortunately for Alexander, he wasn't paid for it.[13]

In March 1783 Alexander and William Paca exchanged correspondence wherein Paca asked Alexander to be as helpful as possible in supplying comfort to prisoners of war, promising like treatment of any British prisoners who might come into Maryland.[14] Paca seems to have understood only too well Alexander's position.

Alexander had to have known he would never be allowed to return to Maryland. His only hope was for the British army to dig deep into its pockets and pay him something for his pain and suffering. This, of course, left him vulnerable to patriots like Paca. Demands could be made, lots of them. Alexander was certainly in no position to refuse, for fear his new benefactor, the British war office, might question his actions.

Alexander's wife, Isabella, was allowed to stay at the family home, The Hermitage, in Cecil County with their six children. There's no evidence she ever saw her husband again, and she apparently spent her time raising her children to be good citizens in the new state. Their eldest son, William, became a prominent lawyer. (In June of 1785, William Paca, by now governor of Maryland, attended graduation ceremonies at Chestertown's Washington College as Lawson Alexander received his degree. The sins of the father apparently weren't imposed on the offspring.)

In England, Alexander set about receiving compensation from the Crown. It helped having the likes of former Royal Governor William Franklin, Ben Franklin's illegitimate son, testifying in his behalf. Another loyalist swearing to his character was James Chalmers. The commandant of the Maryland Loyalists had recently been to Maryland to check on his own properties, and there he met a "Mr. Gorden who lived near Mr. Alexander's Property," who reaffirmed its true value. More importantly for Alexander, he told the commissioners that despite his membership in the Continental Congress, "it was the general opinion of the Loyalists that he was well disposed to this Country and they were well pleased with his being appointed."[15]

England rewarded Alexander well and he lived out his remaining days in comfortable anonymity. London's *Gentleman's Magazine* made the brief observation that he died on November 20, 1805, in his apartments in Norfolk Street, The Strand, aged 64 years.[16] So ended the life of a man who had once risked life and limb getting ammunition and supplies to the colonial resistance—the man who missed his chance to be a signer of the Declaration of Independence.

JAMES CHALMERS

The war may have been over but Chalmers was never one to remain idle. He would soon seek influence again in other theaters of war. For now, though, he tried to settle things at his old home in Kent County.

In May 1785, he wrote to Edward Winslow, the former muster master general of Loyalist forces, in New Brunswick telling him of his journey to Maryland and that he was "now proceed[ing] to England with vouchers of the sale of my Estate, which for this Country may be termed a noble one."[17] Chalmers was lucky the new government wasn't aware to what degree he had plotted its complete destruction.

Had its officials seen the intricate plots he had intended for them, it's unlikely the Maryland loyalist would have been allowed to set foot in the country, much less receive any sort of compensation.

Chalmers wrote his letter to Winslow from New Castle, Delaware, where he had met up with his former junior officer, Walter Dulany. The two were concerned about the status of loyalist land in Maryland. Just a week later, Dulany also wrote to Winslow, hoping to address "the very injurious treatment we have received on account of our Lands."[18]

Chalmers returned to England—not to New Brunswick. The reason may have had to do with the "you snooze, you lose" policy toward claiming lands in New Brunswick. Chalmers lost claim to a piece of land to a Captain Stair Agnew of the Queen's Rangers who used the site to build a sawmill on the Nashwaak River.[19] Chalmers's daughter, Arriana Margaretta, did go to Fredericton, where she married John Saunders, a former Virginian and officer of the Queen's Rangers who became chief justice of the Supreme Court of New Brunswick. Saunders and Chalmers corresponded regularly, and the aging lieutenant colonel's affection for his son-in-law is readily apparent in the dozens of letters preserved at the University of New Brunswick in Fredericton, nearly all of which conclude, "I ever remain Your most affectionate Father & Friend."

Chalmers confided his ambitions, frustrations, and schemes to his son-in-law in the course of nearly twenty years of correspondence. In June 1792, Saunders saw an interesting job opportunity arise in Canada. Edmund Fanning, the lieutenant colonel of Saint John's Island, had suddenly found himself in trouble. The fiery loyalist from North Carolina was charged with tyranny by the citizens of the island of Saint John's (later renamed Prince Edward Island). Sensing an opening to be filled, Saunders encouraged Chalmers to send his memorial to the secretary of state in London. Shortly thereafter, Chalmers told Saunders (rather unconvincingly) that he wasn't disappointed by the man's "total neglect of my pretensions."[20] The Privy Council in England dismissed the charges against Fanning in August and Chalmers's plans, like so many of his others, came to nothing.

By 1796, Chalmers felt the need to compose a pamphlet once again; he wrote it, as he later confessed to Saunders, "when our affairs were at the Lowest."[21] Once again he decided to attack his favorite adversary: Thomas Paine. He also wanted to get in a few words about war with France, the economic history of England, and a nostalgic visit to his own work, *Plain Truth*. His attitudes on Paine hadn't changed much in twenty years:

> His impotence of words and unfounded assertions would excite derision, if the malevolence of his purpose did not incur abhorrence. In this arduous hour, it becomes every good subject to endeavour to expose to public detestation the designs of an incendiary, whose sole aim is to goad and plunge society into dispondency and anarchy.[22]

Strong words. But then, how could any loyalist think otherwise? Paine, more than any single person, had pushed the American rebellion into a full-blown movement for independence.

Chalmers's attitudes toward America seem muted in the pamphlet, almost as if he didn't wish to speak about the new nation. He did, however, see its usefulness in a war against France.

> Such an event will still bind our connexion [connection] closer with America, whose interest, language, and manners, powerfully dispose her to us.—Certainly she ought not, in wisdom, to behold with indifference the vast power of France, who sports with the independence of nations.[23]

He took great pains to establish himself as an Englishman. Finally, though, when the subject of land prices came up, he was reminded of Maryland. With sadness, he noted the sum of money he had received

STRICTURES

ON A

PAMPHLET

Written by Thomas Paine,

ON THE

ENGLISH SYTEM OF FINANCE:

TO WHICH ARE ADDED

SOME REMARKS ON THE WAR,

AND OTHER NATIONAL CONCERNS.

BY *LIEUTENANT-COLONEL CHALMERS,*
OF CHELSEA.

SECOND EDITION.

LONDON:
RE-PRINTED FOR J. DEBRETT, PICCADILLY,
AND J. SEWELL, CORNHILL.
1796.

Even in his declining years, Chalmers was most anxious to square off against his old literary adversary, Thomas Paine: title page of *Strictures*, August 1796. Courtesy British Museum.

for some of his holdings in Kent County, which were, he declared, "richer in natural soil and woods than any beheld from Dijon to the extremity of Scotland."[24]

In short order, he brought up *Plain Truth* with the express purpose of reminding the world at large that he had predicted in 1776 the downfall of the French monarch for his "fatal interference in that contest." As Chalmers pulled out quotes from his old pamphlet, the reader senses the aging Scotsman chuckling in his easy chair with a pronounced attitude of "I told you so!" Referring to himself in the third person, he stated he "wished to bear testimony that, twelve years before the calamities of France, he strained his feeble voice to point out the rocks on which she was madly precipitating herself."[25]

In his final thoughts on the Revolution, he "opposed American Independence because he thought it premature, because he believed, that if precipitated, it would occasion great evils to America, to Great Britain, and the rest of Europe."[26]

Writing did not, however, occupy all his time. The aging former Marylander gathered up his sword and sash and signed on for active military service once again in 1797 as inspector general of colonial troops in the West Indies. His commander was another former loyalist officer, Major General John Simcoe. Writing to Saunders from Port au Prince, Haiti, in July, Chalmers expressed his disappointment with Simcoe, who had failed to keep a promise with regard to his half-pay. In a huff, Chalmers then resigned. Boarding a boat for America, he took yet another trip to Maryland to attempt to put his holdings in order before stopping off for a visit with his daughter and son-in-law in Fredericton.[27]

His service with the British army concluded, Chalmers retired once again to London, moved into a house in Chelsea with his wife and family, and collected half-pay from the government. Age may have stopped him from service in the field but he still had plenty of ideas and suggestions which he was determined to share with his fellow Englishmen.

Chalmers's pen was seldom put aside for long. His final publication came in November 1804. *Remarks on the late War in St. Domingo; with Observations on the relative Situation of Jamaica, and other interesting Subjects* was reviewed favorably by London's *Gentleman's Magazine*, which called Chalmers "an officer of great experience." Meditating on England's military failures in the West Indies, Chalmers was ready to contribute his thoughts to the subject. Ever the armchair general, he stated, "If the proposal of General Simcoe, to return immediately with a few thousand troops, aided by French Loyalists, to the accomplishment of the reduction of French St. Domingo, had been acceded to, its success would have been infallible."[28]

Chalmers spent his remaining days entertaining prominent loyalist friends like former Royal Governor William Franklin and Edward Winslow when the latter visited London in 1805.[29] There seems to be no record of any correspondence with his former Maryland Loyalist officers. Even William Augustus Bowles on his numerous trips to London apparently never visited his old commander.

The end came on October 4, 1806, when Chalmers died from dropsy at No. 12 Paradise Row, the London home of his son, Alexander Jekyll Chalmers, a major in the Fifty-fifth Regiment of Foot. *Gentleman's Magazine* was generous in its remarks:

> Col. C[halmer]'s military talents were tried and honourably acknowledged. . . . His literary powers were respectable; the many political compositions he published, in America and in England, are replete with British loyalty, and evince much shrewdness and originality of thought.[30]

Two months later, Chalmers's son-in-law wrote to Alexander saying, "I have no doubt but that the cause of his disease originated in the mind and that he has fallen a martyr to his feelings."[31] The grand schemer was gone. One small thread of the fabric of the American Revolution was consigned to oblivion.

Epilogue

In 1940, author Kenneth Roberts's loyalist historical novel *Oliver Wiswell* was published. Roberts, best known as the author of *Northwest Passage*, told the story of the fictional title character, a young loyalist caught up in the turmoil of the Revolution. In the course of his trials and tribulations, he encounters real-life loyalists such as Edward Winslow, Ward Chipman, and General Simcoe. The book also made what must be the only literary reference ever to the Maryland Loyalists.

At the conclusion of the story, Wiswell makes his way to New Brunswick in 1783. Once there, Colonel Winslow informs him of the terrible shipwreck of the *Martha* and the loss of men, women, and children from DeLancey's Brigade and the Maryland Loyalists. Winslow adds that he heard the story directly from Dr. Stafford, the regimental surgeon of the Maryland Loyalists. Although the story repeats verbatim some of the sworn testimony of the Provincial officers concerning the wreck, the author took the literary license of allowing Colonel Chalmers to go down with the ship. The real life Chalmers probably would have said, "Don't change the ending!"

This brief mention of the tragedy, though, has stood alone. No songs were ever sung about the *Martha*, although the story was certainly the stuff sad songs are made of. Today, visitors to Upton House in Warwickshire, England, gaze at the portrait of William Augustus Bowles on display, intrigued by his rakish good looks. Few can suspect the story lurking behind the handsome blue eyes.

Because the First Battalion of Maryland Loyalists fought on the wrong side, they were banished. Because they didn't shed blood at the great battles of the Revolution, they were forgotten. One author, noting their small numbers, called them a "paper unit." It was a superficial, but typical assessment. It is doubtful that the Maryland Loyalists who dodged cannonballs at the siege of Pensacola felt they belonged to a "paper unit."

Only a few names are remembered from the Revolution: George Washington, Benedict Arnold, Charles Cornwallis. Others who greatly influenced the war are less well known. All the rest simply lived through one of history's great moments without recognition. They put their muskets back over the fireplace and quietly rebuilt their lives when the war ended. This is certainly the story of the Maryland Loyalists.

Appendix

First Muster Rolls of the Maryland Loyalists, Philadelphia, 1777

Return of First Battalion of Mary[land] Loyalists Commanded by Lieut. Colonel James Chalmers, November 26, 1777. (National Archives of Canada, RG 8, "C" Series, Volume 1904, Page 13)

    1 lieutenant colonel, 1 major, 3 captains, 3 lieutenants, 3 ensigns, 1 quarter master, 1 surgeon, 1 surgeon's mate, 3 serjeants, 116 privates.

Lieut. Col. James Chalmers
Major John McDonald
Captains Grafton Dulany, Alexander Middleton, and Patrick Kennedy
Lieutenants Walter Dulany, Esqr., James Inglis, and Thomas Boswell
Ensigns Allen, McPherson, and Dewirtz (?)
Qr. Master Mr. Joseph Garnett
Surgeon William Sinclair
Surgeon's Mate Mr.——Dalton

                                    [Signed] James Chalmers
                                              Lieut. Colonel

GRAFTON DULANY'S CO.

Muster Roll of Grafton Dulany's Company of the First Battalion of Maryland Loyalists commanded by Lieutenant Colonel James Chalmers, Philadelphia, November 25, 1777. (National Archives of Canada, RG 8, "C" Series, Volume 1904, Page 14)

Name	Date Enlisted	Recruiting Officer	Status/Condition
Lieut. Colonel James Chalmers	14 Octr. 1777		
Major John McDonald	11 Novr. 1777		
Captain Grafton Dulany			
Lieutenant Boswell			
Ensign [blank]			
Adjutant [blank]			
Surgeon [blank]			
Mate [blank]			
Qr. Master [blank]			
Sgt. Thomas Welch		Capt. Dulany	
Sgt. George Fettyplace	(?)	Lt. Inglis	
Sgt. John Selby	25 Novr. 1777	Capt. Jones	
Peter Lanute	15 Novr. 1777	Capt. Dulany	
Lawrence Messit	do*	do	
Joseph Davenport	do	do	
Charles Harter	do	do	
Cornelius Farrel	do	do	
John Rhodes	do	do	
George Wilkinson	do	do	
John Stone	do	do	
Alexander Swindle	do	do	
Terence Hughs	do	do	
David Neily	do	do	
Abraham Shelly	do	do	
Joseph Talent	do	do	
Jacob Rogers	25 Novr. 1777	Capt. Jones	
Thomas Calhan	do	do	
John White	do	do	
Zachariah Pain	do	do	
Southy Sterling	do	do	

* Ditto

Name	Date Enlisted	Recruiting Officer	Status/Condition
Thomas Buker	do*	do	
Joshua Merril	do	do	
Robert Story	do	do	
Henry Chassey	do	do	
Michael O'Neil	do	do	
John Brown	15 Novr. 1777	Lt. Boswell	
John Brown, Junr.	do	do	Sick
Thomas Page	25 Octr. 1777	do	
William Warren	14 Novr. 1777	do	
John Dennis	13 Novr. 1777	do	Sick
James King	14 Novr. 1777	do	do
James Kirkwood	23 Novr. 1777	do	
William Fitzpatrick	25 Novr. 1777	Capt. Jones	Discharged 26 Novr. 1777 by the Inspector General
John Dickenson	6 Novr. 1777	——Anderson	
James Doneville	1 Novr. 1777	do	Sick
Thomas Gratton	4 Novr. 1777	do	
Benjamin Chrezot	26 Novr. 1777	do	
John Powell	13 Novr. 1777	——Dewitz	
James Carrol	do	do	
Michael Durt			

CAPTAIN MIDDLETON'S CO.

Muster Roll of Captain Alexander Middleton's Company of the First Battalion of Maryland Loyalists, Commanded by Lieut. Col. James Chalmers, Philadelphia, November 25, 1777. (National Archives of Canada, RG 8, "C" Series, Volume 1904, Page 18)

Name	Date Enlisted	Recruiting Officer	Status/Condition
Captain Alexander Middleton	27 Octr. 1777		
Lieutenant James Inglis			
Ensign Adam Allen			
Sgt. Patrick Dowing	10 Novr. 1777	Lt. Inglis	
Sgt. George Fettyplace	6 Octr. 1777		

---

* Ditto

Name	Date Enlisted	Recruiting Officer	Status/Condition
Frederick Hitner	30 Octr. 1777	Capt. Middleton	Sick
William Camell	1 Novr. 1777	do*	do
John Friday	do	do	
Patrick Callahan	2 Novr. 1777	do	
Daniel McCarty	do	do	
John Williams	do	do	
William McFarrin	do	do	Sick
Francis Lithiff	12 Novr. 1777	do	
John Beller	14 do	do	
Thomas Whitaire	19 do	do	
William Collins	20 do	do	
Hugh McLure	26 do	do	
John Wilkinson	do	do	
Michael Nowel	do	do	
John McKinley	do	do	
William Prowce	do	do	
Thomas Williams	19 Novr. 1777	Ens. Allen	Sick
James Gilmore	do	do	
George Fittiplace†	6 do	Lt. Englis	
Andrew Spaldwin	do	do	
Antony Flout	13 do	do	
Joseph Coast	do	do	
William Laird	20 do	do	Deserted 24 Novr. 1777
John Moore	do	do	
William Howe	do	do	
Dominick Fishback	27 Octr. 1777	Capt. Middleton	Deserted 1 Novr. 1777
Daniel McMullen	1 Novr. 1777	do	Deserted 22 Novr. 1777
Peter Higgins	do	do	do

CAPTAIN KENNEDY'S CO.

Muster Roll of Captain Patrick Kennedy's company of the First Battalion of Maryland Loyalists, Commanded by Lieutenant Colonel James Chalmers, Philadelphia, November 25, 1777. (National Archives of Canada, RG 8, "C" Series, Volume 1904, Page 15)

---

* Ditto

† Fettyplace

Appendix

Name	Date Enlisted	Recruiting Officer	Status/Condition
Captain Patrick Kennedy			
Lieutenant Walter Dulany			
Ensign John McPherson			
Sgt John Dunbar	6 Novr. 1777	Capt. Kennedy	
Sgt Arthur Campbell	do*	do	
Patrick Butler		do	
David Humphreys	6 Novr. 1777	do	
Abraham Hazelton	do	do	Deserted 26 Novr. 1777
James McDonald, Sr.	do	do	
James McDonald, Jr.	do	do	
James Welldon	do	do	
Thomas Gray	do	do	
Samuel Johnston, Sr.	do	do	Deserted 25 Novr. 1777
Patrick McAnelly	do	do	
John Callaghan	do	do	Deserted 25 Novr. 1777
Joseph Carrol	do	do	
Redmond McDonagh	do	do	
Thomas Prust	do	do	
John Powell	do	do	
John Moore	do	do	Sickness in Quarters
Frederick Bechan	do	do	
William Griffin	do	do	
Henry Main	do	do	
John Stephens	do	do	
James Cummings	do	do	
Archibald Taylor	do	do	
Sylvester McCarty	do	do	
Bernard Forster	do	do	
John Rutliff	do	do	
Simeon Humphreys	do	do	
Jesse Hall	do	do	
Patrick Carrol, Sr.	do	do	
Fergus McCleod	do	do	
Michael Cross	do	do	Sickness in Hospital
John McClean	do	do	Absent at muster but since retd.
Thomas Conolly	do	do	
Peter O'Neil	do	do	

* Ditto

Name	Date Enlisted	Recruiting Officer	Status/Condition
Samuel Johnston, Jr.	do*	do	
William Gray	do	do	
John Carrol	do	do	
John Kelly	do	do	
John Sullivan	do	do	
William Smith	do	do	
Moses Lock	do	do	
David Williams	do	do	
John King	do	do	Deserted 27 Novr. 1777
Bryan Carrol	do	do	
Christopher Brady	do	do	
Patrick Carrol, Jr.	do	do	
Thomas Hand	do	do	
Daniel Carty	do	do	
Jacob Ringle	do	do	
John Copper	do	do	
John Dawn	6 Novr. 1777	Capt. Kennedy	
Matthias Waggoner	do	do	
Thomas Logan	do	do	
Drummer Jacob Rosewell	do	do	

The Final Muster Rolls, New York, 1783

CAPTAIN JONES'S CO.

Muster Roll of Captain Caleb Jones's Company of the 1st Battalion of Maryland Loyalists, James Chalmers, Esqr., Lieutenant Colonel Commandant, Denyce's, [blank] of August, 1783. (National Archives of Canada, RG 8, "C" Series, Volume 1904, Page 5)

Name	Status/Condition
Captain Caleb Jones	
Sgt Zachariah Bailey	
Sgt John White	
Sgt Robert Harris	

---
* Ditto

Name	Status/Condition
Sgt John Noble	Promoted 30 July 1783
Cpl James Love	do* do
Drummer John Clemons	
Thomas Steeples	
Cornelius Murphey	
George Matthews	
John Conklin	
Joshua Walston	
Joseph Newbourne	
Thomas Irvin	
Henry White	
John Cotton	Dead 15 July 1783
John Gray	Discharged 20 July 1783—gone to Europe

CAPTAIN TOWNSEND'S CO.

Muster Roll of Captain Levin Townsend's Company in the Maryland Loyalists, James Chalmers, Esqr., Lieut. Col. Commandant, August 1783. (National Archives of Canada, RG 8, "C" Series, Volume 1904, Page 6)

Name	Status/Condition
Captain Levin Townsend	In England by leave
Lieutenant William Sterling	
Sgt John Morgan	
Cpl James McComb	
Drummer Dennis Calagan	
Charles Morgan	
Charles Harter	
Daniel McEvoy	
George Wilkenson	On Guard
Thomas Carrol	
Allen Morrison	
John Carol	On Guard
Lawrence Messit	
James King	

---

* Ditto

Name	Status/Condition
Joseph Fallent	
John Malone	On Guard
Ambrose Miles	do*
Daniel Fukes†	

The following October dates are obviously wrong as the unit was already in Nova Scotia. A number of those men drowned when the regiment was shipwrecked.

CAPTAIN KENNEDY'S CO.

Muster Roll of Captain Kennedy's Company in the Regt. of Maryland Loyalists Whereof James Chalmers is Lieutenant Colonel Commandant, Denyses, October 1783. (National Archives of Canada, RG 8, "C" Series, Volume 1904, Page 1)

Name	Status/Condition
Lt. Col. James Chalmers	
Major Walter Dulaney	
Captain Patrick Kennedy	Sick in New York
Ensign William A. Bowles	With Leave in New York
Ensign Thomas Gill	Promoted 30 July 1783
Adjutant James Henley	in Sick Quarters
Quarter Master Thomas Welch	With Leave in Nova Scotia
Surgeon William Stafford	
Chaplain John Paterson	
Sgt Joshua Merrill	
Sgt Jacob Rogers	
Sgt Isaac Cullin	
Cpl Cannon Rigin	
Drummer Robert Keer	
Joseph Carrel	
Patrick Butler	

---

* Ditto

† According to Wright's *Loyalists of New Brunswick*, Daniel Fukes's name, among others, shows up on a land grant of 13,750 acres (known as Block 1) across the river from St. Ann's (Fredericton), New Brunswick, July 14, 1784.

Name	Status/Condition
John Ratlif	Deserted 16 July 1783
Moses Lock	
Matthyas Waggoner	
James Cummins	
Nicholas Brock	With leave in New York
Simon Umphris	
John Dunbar	
John Urquert	On Duty in New York
Forgay McCloud	
James McDonald	
William Kelley	
Frederick Beham	

CAPTAIN KEY'S CO.

Muster Roll of Captain Key's Company in the Regiment of Maryland Loyalists, whereof Lieut. Colonel James Chalmers is Commandant, October 1783. (National Archives of Canada, RG 8, "C" Series, Volume 1904, Page 2)

Name	Status/Condition
Captain Philip Key	With Leave in England
Lieutenant James Henley	Sick in Quarters
Sgt Lemuel Cohee	Promoted 17 Augt. 1783
Sgt George Fettiplace	Sick in New York
Sgt James Cohee	
Cpl William Savage	At New Town, Promoted 22 Augt. 1783
William Wells	On guard
Samuel Woodard	Promoted 22 Augt. 1783
Patrick Harvey	
John Shaddock	
John Owens	Sick in Hospital
Samuel Rogers	
Matthew Bennett	
William Baynerd	On the Provision Store Guard
Thomas Young	
David Clark	
Finley Munro	

Name	Status/Condition
Joseph White	On duty in New York
John Stephens	Deserted 16 July 1783

CAPTAIN ADDISON'S CO.

Muster Roll of Captain Addison's Company in the Regiment of Maryland Loyalists whereof James Chalmers is Lieut.Colonel Commandant, October 1783. (National Archives of Canada, RG 8, "C" Series, Volume 1904, Page 4)

Name	Status/Condition
Captain Daniel Dulany Addison	
Ensign John Stewart	In New York
Sgt Hugh Dimond	Dead 4 July 1783
Cpl Mark McCausland	
William Morrice	
John Friday	
Jacob Ramson	
Thomas Clay	Sick

CAPTAIN STERLING'S CO.

Muster Roll of Captain Sterling's Company of the Regiment of Maryland Loyalists whereof James Chalmers Esqr. is Lieutenant Colonel Commandant, Denyses, October 1783. (National Archives of Canada, RG 8, "C" Series, Volume 1904, Page 3)

Name	Status/Condition
Captain John Sterling	Promoted 16 July 1783
Ensign John Chalmers	Absent by Leave in England
Ensign Levin Vaughan	Promoted 30 July 1783
Sgt William Owans	
Sgt Thomas Ingles	Absent by Leave in Maryland
Cpl Ephraim Cottingham	
Cpl Robert Skinner	Promoted 11 Augt. 1783 Guard
William Savage	Promoted 22 Augt. 1783 and Transfer'd Into Captain Keys' Co.
Isaac Harriss	

Name	Status/Condition
Stephen Beachamp	
Richard Couple	Deserted 11 July 1783
John Mitchall	
Hue McDonald	
Robert King	
Benjamin B[utler?]	
James [torn]	[torn]
[torn]	Absent by Leave in Maryland
[torn]	Sick
[torn]	Absent by Leave in Maryland
[torn] Johnston [Richard Johnson?]	
Henry Chesey	
John Williams	
John Cayton	

Reported Deaths

No comprehensive list of Maryland Loyalist deaths or desertions has ever been published. Poring over muster rolls for this information is extremely tedious and time-consuming, yet it reveals much about the circumstances of the unit itself.

Over the course of several years of muster rolls, names frequently were misspelled. Alternative spellings have been included when deemed appropriate. (National Archives of Canada, RG 8, "C" Series, Volumes 1904-1905; compiled by the author.)

Name	Enlisted	Died
Dulany's Co., 1778		
Godfrey Oxford	3 Decr. 1777	28 Decr. 1777
Kennedy's Co., February 24, 1778.		
William Gray	6 Novr. 1777	10 Feby. 1778
Jones's Co., July 11, 1778.		
Benjamin Shockley	26 March 1778	27 May 1778

Name	Enlisted	Died
COSTEN'S CO., JULY 11, 1778.		
Solomon Denston	1 March 1778	27 June 1778
FRISBY'S CO., JULY 11, 1778.		
Thomas Baker	15 Novr. 1777	18 May 1778
COSTEN'S CO., SEPTEMBER 4, 1778.		
Elijah Jones	1 May 1778	15 July 1778
COSTEN'S CO., OCTOBER, 14, 1778.		
Jonathon Cottingham	1 May 1778	Sept/Oct. 1778
Elisha Nickleson	1 May 1778	Sept/Oct. 1778
Sgt James Tull	1 May 1778	Sept/Oct. 1778
JONES'S CO., OCTOBER 14, 1778.		
Thomas White	1 March 1778	Sept/Oct. 1778
COSTEN'S CO. FEBRUARY 22, 1779.		
William Robison [Robertson]	1 May 1778	20 Feby. 1779
Jacob Riggin	1 May 1778	8 Feby. 1779
Levi Cottingham	1 May 1778	1 Feby. 1779
Thomas Benston	1 May 1778	3 Feby. 1779
Levin Green	1 May 1778	9 Feby. 1779
James Harris	1 May 1778	4 Feby. 1779
George Dorman	1 May 1778	7 Feby. 1779
Elisha Cottingham	1 May 1778	1 Feby. 1779
Joseph Cottman	1 May 1778	5 Feby. 1779
Thomas Hall	1 May 1778	12 Jany. 1779
Nathaniel Smulling	1 May 1778	2 Feby. 1779
Levi Wood[s]	1 May 1778	20 Jany. 1779
Henry Miles	1 May 1778	3 Feby. 1779
Henry Whaley	1 May 1778	7 Feby. 1779
David Hayman	1 May 1778	16 Feby. 1779
George Evans	1 May 1778	16 Feby. 1779
Cpl Randolph Smulling	do*	5 Feby. 1779

* Ditto

Name	Enlisted	Died
KENNEDY'S CO., FEBRUARY 23, 1779.		
Surgeon Alexander Kidd	?	Decr. 1778
Thomas Holmes	10 Sept. 1777	15 Novr. 1778
JONES'S CO., FEBRUARY 22, 1779.		
William Pepper	1 March 1778	26 Jany. 1779
Nathan Thornton	1 April 1778	28 Jany. 1779
Leven Costen [Coston]	26 March 1778	11 Feby. 1779
Noble Sullivan	26 March 1778	3 Feby. 1779
Curtis Bosman [Bozman]	1 April 1778	3 Feby. 1779
James Dykes	26 March 1778	5 Feby. 1779
Benjamin Summers	1 March 1778	5 Feby. 1779
Benjamin Driggers	26 March 1778	5 Feby. 1779
Richard Dicks	1 March 1778	7 Feby. 1779
Zachariah Payne	25 Novr. 1777	8 Feby. 1779
Samuel Beal	1 March 1778	18 Feby. 1779
Obadiah Smith [Cpl Obediah Smith]	23 Jany. 1778	2 Feby. 1779
KEY'S CO., FEBRUARY 22, 1779.		
William Ogan	18 March 1778	15 Jany. 1779
James Dyer	1 May 1778	19 Feby. 1779
Isaac Jones	?	27 Decr. 1778
FRISBY'S CO., FEBRUARY 22, 1779.		
Francis Obeir	21 March 1778	1 Feby. 1779
Isaac Tutt	26 Feby. 1778	1 Feby. 1779
Henry Prattman	7 March 1778	6 Feby. 1779
Joseph Dickinson [Joshua Dickenson]	26 March 1778	23 Jany. 1779
DULANY'S CO., FEBRUARY 23, 1779.		
Captain Grafton Dulany	25 Novr. 1777	27 Decr. 1778
Cpl Stephen Bootman [Boatman]	18 Decr. 1777	4 Febr. 1779
KENNEDY'S CO., APRIL 26, 1779.		
Sgt Thomas Wilson	6 Novr. 1777	29 March 1779

Name	Enlisted	Died
COSTEN'S CO., AUGUST 25, 1779.		
Daniel Shay	25 Octr. 1778	19 Augt. 1779
COSTEN'S CO., OCTOBER 25, 1779.		
Benjamin Crezit [Crizett]	26 Novr. 1777	2 Octr. 1779
James Carrol	13 Novr. 1777	11 Octr. 1779
CAPTAIN KEARNEY'S OF THE INVALID COMPANY OF THE UNITED CORPS OF THE PENNSYLVANIA AND MARYLAND LOYALISTS COMMANDED BY LIEUT. COL. WILLIAM ALLEN (PENNSYLVANIA LOYALISTS), FEBRUARY 25, 1780.		
Sgt Patrick Downing	10 Novr. 1777	7 Jany. 1780
John Ryan	3 Jany. 1778	7 Jany. 1780
William Brown	9 Febr. 1778	7 Jany. 1780
William Appleby [Applebee]	17 March 1778	14 Jany. 1780
James Quin	4 March 1778	14 Jany. 1780
John Twells [Twils or Twell]	17 Feby. 1778	19 Jany. 1780
Daniel Stuart	7 April 1778	23 Feby. 1780
CAPTAIN WALTER DULANY'S COMPANY IN THE UNITED CORPS OF PENNSYLVANIA & MARYLAND LOYALISTS, COMMANDED BY LIEUT. COL. WILLIAM ALLEN, PENSACOLA, FEBRUARY 25, 1780.		
Sgt Patrick Downing	see above	see above
Daniel Carty	6 Novr. 1777	18 Jany. 1780
CAPTAIN KEARNEY'S CO., UNITED CORPS, APRIL 25, 1780.		
John McKinley [McKinly]	26 Novr. 1777	27 March 1780
John Smith	?	1 March 1780
James Welding [Wheldon?]	6 Novr. 1777	16 April 1780
CAPTAIN WALTER DULANEY'S CO., UNITED CORPS, PENSACOLA, APRIL 25, 1780.		
Volunteer William C. Dallas	?	8 April 1780
James Dilworth [Delworth]	18 March 1778	8 April 1780
CAPTAIN JONES'S COMPANY OF THE UNITED CORPS OF PENNSYLVANIA & MARYLAND LOYALISTS COMMANDED BY LIEUT. COL. WILLIAM ALLEN COMMANDER, PENSACOLA, APRIL 25, 1780.		
Samuel Gray	1 March 1778	5 March 1780
WALTER DULANEY'S CO., JULY 14, 1781.		
Mark Dogherty [Dougherty]	16 Decr. 1777	18 June 1781

Appendix

Name	Enlisted	Died
Captain Jones's Co., October 24, 1781.		
Benjamin Gray	21 March 1778	3 Octr. 1781
William Lovell [Lovewell]	15 Decr. 1777	21 Octr. 1781
John Townsend	26 March 1778	14 Octr. 1781
Captain Frisby's Co., October 24, 1781.		
Michael O'Neil	25 Novr. 1777	24 Octr. 1781
Captain Kennedy's Co., December 24, 1781.		
Ens William Jones*	Jan. 1780?	Dead—no date
Captain Jones's Co., December 24, 1781.		
Archibald Campbell	1 March 1778	24 Jany. 1782
Henry Hallworth [Halworth]	15 Decr. 1777	28 Octr. 1781
Captain Jones's Co., April 25, 1782.		
Andrew Brown	8 Jany. 1778	7 April 1782
Captain Daniel Dulany Addison's Co., October 25, 1782.		
James Coland		11 Augt. 1782
Captain Frisby's Co., March 5, 1783.		
John Cash	10 April 1778	13 Feby. 1783
Captain Kennedy's Co., March 5, 1783.		
Simon Humphreys [Simeon Humphrys]	6 Novr. 1777	15 Novr. 1782
John Orchard	20 Decr. 1777	15 Novr. 1782
Captain Jones's Co., August, 1783.		
John Cotton	25 Decr. 1777	15 July 1783
Captain Addison's Co., October, 1783.		
Sgt Hugh Dimond [John][Diamond]†	29 Novr. 1777	4 July 1783

Total reported deaths: 84

* The previous ensign in Kennedy's company was William Augustus Bowles, who resigned at Pensacola on March 28, 1779.

† Sergeant Dimond is the last reported death in the muster rolls. It is tragic that, as one of the earliest recruits to the unit, he survived smallpox and Spanish cannon balls, only to die just a few months before the dwindling unit shipped off to Canada. The ironic date of his death should also be noted.

Desertions

The Maryland Loyalists suffered a very large number of desertions —very close to half the total number who served. Considering some of their dire circumstances, it's a wonder there weren't more. More than a few of these men later joined the Continental Army. Should the reader spot a revered Revolutionary War ancestor on these deserter rolls, bear in mind that good or bad, they are all equal now. (National Archives of Canada, RG 8, "C" Series, Volumes 1904-1905; compiled by the author.)

Name	Enlisted	Deserted
Captain Alexander Middleton's Co., November 25, 1777.		
William Laird*	20 Novr. 1777	24 Novr. 1777
Dominick Fishback	27 Octr. 1777	21 Novr. 1777
Daniel McMullen	1 Novr. 1777	22 Novr. 1777
Peter Higgins	1 Novr. 1777	22 Novr. 1777
Kennedy's Co., February 25, 1777.		
Abraham Hazleton	6 Novr. 1777	26 Novr. 1777
Samuel Johnston, Sr.†	6 Novr. 1777	25 Novr. 1777
John Callaghan	6 Novr. 1777	25 Novr. 1777
John King	6 Novr. 1777	27 Novr. 1777
Grafton Dulany's Co., [1778]		
William Berry	29 Novr. 1777	29 Decr. 1777
Frederic Heborly	14 Decr. 1777	2 Jany. 1778
Middleton's Co., January 19, 1778.		
Jeremiah Heath	16 Decr. 1777	17 Jany. 1778
Grafton Dulany's Co., February 24, 1778.		
William Warren	14 Novr. 1777	20 Jany. 1778
John Anderson	11 Decr. 1777	20 Jany. 1778
William Marsial	10 Decr. 1777	24 Feby. 1778

* Obviously, army life didn't agree with Mr. Laird since his stay with the Maryland Loyalists was a mere four days. It would appear that Mr. McMullen and Mr. Higgins joined together and deserted together.

† Strangely, Samuel Johnston, Jr., who was in the same company, did not desert with his father. What must family reunions have been like for the Johnston family?

Name	Enlisted	Deserted
KENNEDY'S CO., FEBRUARY 24, 1778.		
Patrick McAnelly	6 Novr. 1777	27 Feby. 1778
Jacob Ringler	6 Novr. 1777	27 Feby. 1778
Thomas Hand	do*	do
Thomas Conolly	do	10 Jany. 1778
JONES'S CO., FEBRUARY 24, 1778.		
John McMahon	30 Decr. 1777	20 Feby. 1778
John Shepard	2 Jany. 1777	do
WALTER DULANY'S CO., FEBRUARY 24, 1778.		
Kenan Purcell	26 Decr. 1777	10 Feby. 1778
James Byrns	21 Decr. 1777	31 Jany. 1778
GRAFTON DULANY'S CO., JULY 11, 1778.		
Thomas Page	26 Octr. 1777	30 June 1778
John Ross	1 Jany. 1778	3 July 1778
John Stone	6 Novr. 1777	24 June 1778
KENNEDY'S CO., JULY 11, 1778.		
Sgt Arthur Campbell	6 Novr. 1777	Deserted to the Rebels 24 June 1778
Michael Cross	6 Novr. 1777	Deserted to the Rebels 24 June 1778
James Weldon†	6 Novr. 1777	Deserted to the Rebels 24 June 1778
David Williams	do	do
George Leadbeater	20 Decr. 1777	do
JONES'S CO., JULY 11, 1778.		
Robert Story	25 Novr. 1777	15 May 1778
Littleton Abdell	26 March 1778	30 May 1778
James Wallace	1 March 1778	5 June 1778
Elisha Taylor	do	20 June 1778
John Charnock	do	do
Abel Charnock	do	do
Sgt John Selby	25 Novr. 1777	4 July 1778
Southy Sterling	do	do
John White, Jr.‡	1 March 1778	do
Henry Clark	26 do	do

---

* Ditto

† The fact of Mr. Weldon's desertion could be a mistake, since he seems to have died in the unit in 1780.

‡ Two other Whites, Henry and Thomas, enlisted on the same day as John White, Jr.

Name	Enlisted	Deserted
William Simpson	1 March 1778	do*
William Cameron	do	do
Andrew McCruady	do	do

WALTER DULANY'S CO., JULY 12, 1778.

William Griffin	6 Novr. 1777	Deserted to the Rebels 24 June 1778

KEY'S CO., JULY 11, 1778.

Cpl John Fleming	4 March 1777	Claimed as a deserter by the Queen's Rangers 16 June 1778

COSTEN'S CO., JULY 11, 1778.

Sgt Horatio Stayten	1 March 1778	26 June 1778
Cpl William Selbey	do	4 July 1778
Daniel Eshon	do	do
Daniel Sellby	do	4 June 1778
John Parker	do	do
Thomas Parker	do	do
William McDaniel	do	do
Job Newton	do	do†

FRISBY'S CO., JULY 11, 1778.

Bryan Byrnes	1 May 1778	26 June 1778
Elisha Osbourn	20 Decr. 1777	16 June 1778
Thomas Mitchell	17 March 1778	do
Solomon Colbourn	4 March 1778	do
James Rowle	20 May 1778	do
John Mitchell	16 March 1778	do
Jacob Welman	27 Feby. 1778	do
Thomas Wright	25 Decr. 1777	do
John Campbell	16 Feby. 1778	do
James Campbell	do	do

KENNEDY'S CO., SEPTEMBER 4, 1778.

Christopher Brady	6 Novr. 1777	18 Augt. 1778
Thomas Logan	6 Novr. 1777	18 Augt. 1778
Redmond McDonagh	do	9 Augt. 1778

---

* Ditto

† Deserting solo was not something these Marylanders practiced.

Name	Enlisted	Deserted
GRAFTON DULANY'S CO., SEPTEMBER 4, 1778.		
Andrew Nelson	27 March 1778	6 Augt. 1778
Abraham Shelly	6 Novr. 1778	do*
John Brown	13 Novr. 1778	do
John Brown, Jr.	11 April 1778	do
Robert Kespolt	14 Decr. 1777	3 Augt. 1778
Alexander Swindle	6 Novr. 1778	6 Augt. 1778
Barnet Turner	25 Decr. 1777	8 Augt. 1778
James Donavan	4 Novr. 1777	do
WALTER DULANY'S CO., SEPTEMBER 4, 1778.		
John McKinly†	26 Novr. 1777	8 Augt. 1778
Thomas Quixell	29 Decr. 1777	25 July 1778
William Saunders	10 Decr. 1777	Deserted [no date]
Andrew Rankins	23 Decr. 1777	do
KEY'S CO., SEPTEMBER 4, 1778.		
Samuel Carlisle	27 April 1778	12 Augt. 1778
John Curry	do	do
FRISBY'S CO., SEPTEMBER 4, 1778.		
Sgt Elisha Dickenson	7 March 1778	23 Augt. 1778
Henry Murphy	11 March 1778	do
Oliver Johnston	9 April 1778	do
COSTEN'S CO., SEPTEMBER 4, 1778.‡		
Cpl William Selby	1 May 1778	4 July 1778
Daniel Eshon	do	do
Samuel Miles	do	15 Augt. 1778
Daniel Selby	do	4 June 1778
John Floyd	do	15 Augt. 1778
Levin Tull	do	do
Henry Selbey	do	do
John Parker	do	4 June 1778
Thomas Parker	do	do
Selby Newton	do	15 Augt. 1778

---

* Ditto

† McKinly seems to have died at Pensacola in 1780. Did he desert and come back?

‡ Costen's company seems to have had a curse on it—first beset by many desertions in New York, then the hardest hit by the smallpox in Florida.

Name	Enlisted	Deserted
William McDonald	do*	4 June 1778
Job Newton	do	24 Augt. 1778
William Cauley	do	do

GRAFTON DULANY'S CO., OCTOBER 14, 1778.

Abram [Abraham] Shelly	6 Novr. 1777	Deserted & Inlisted in ye [British] Legion, an Officer of which took him from a Sgt who was bringing him to the Regt.

WALTER DULANY'S CO., OCTOBER 14, 1778.

Andrew Spaldwin [Spalding]†	6 Novr. 1777	Deserted before last muster—Said to be Inlisted in the Legion C. McKinseys Cmpy.

WALTER DULANY'S CO., FEBRUARY 22, 1779, PENSACOLA FL

Francis Lettiff‡	20 Novr. 1777	24 Augt. 1778
John Reed	21 Feby. 1778	2 Decr. 1778
George Foster [Forster]	31 Decr. 1777	11 Decr. 1778
Cpl Daniel Gill	29 Novr. 1777	16 Decr. 1778
Peter McCoard [McCord]	31 Decr. 1777	do

JONES'S CO., FEBRUARY 22, 1779.

James Marr	15 Decr. 1777	24 Decr. 1778

GRAFTON DULANY'S CO., FEBRUARY 22, 1779.

Thomas Gratton	4 Novr. 1777	25 Octr. 1778

JONES'S CO., FEBRUARY 22, 1779.

Peter [Porter] Brown§	2 April 1778	15 March 1779

---

* Ditto

† It would be hard to track down a deserter if one didn't have his correct name.

‡ On the September 17, 1778, rolls, Mr. Lettiff is listed as being on board the brig *William*. It's unclear whether he made his escape before or after being taken to the prison ship.

§ Presumably, this is the same man who tried to desert in the summer of 1778 and returned on August 24, 1778. The orderly book of the regiment kept by Captain Jones refers to Brown's sentence of 500 lashes for desertion on September 12, 1778. Mr. Brown apparently remained patient, however, and waited for the right opportunity to try again. This time he succeeded.

Name	Enlisted	Deserted
FRISBY'S CO., APRIL 26, 1779.		
John McKenny [McKennie]*	11 March 1778	14 March 1779
Richard Copple	10 April 1778	do†
WALTER DULANY'S CO., APRIL 26, 1779.		
William Morris‡	1 May 1778	14 March 1779
Richard Morris‡	do	do
George Barcus‡	do	do
Lewis Barcus‡	do	do
Oliver Johnson	9 April 1778	do
Isaac Burbridge	31 Decr. 1777	do
John Moor [Moore]	6 Decr. 1777	do
James Robison	?	do
COSTEN'S CO., APRIL 25, 1779.		
Sgt Philip Condon [Conden]§	8 Decr. 1777	14 March 1779; 2 April 1779, Delivered himself up to Capt. Christie
John McGlaughlan [McLocklin]§	10 Decr. 1777	14 March 1779
KENNEDY'S CO., UNITED CORPS, FEBRUARY 25, 1780.		
James Kelly#	17 Decr. 1777	15 Feby. 1780
KEY'S CO., UNITED CORPS, APRIL 25, 1780.		
Philip Conden**	8 Decr. 1777	15 March 1780
Jonathon Watkins	1 April 1778	do

---

* It is worthy of note that McKenny in July of 1778 was listed as a guard for the commander in chief, Sir Henry Clinton—quite an honorable post.

† Ditto

‡ Never let it be said Maryland families don't stay together.

§ Sergeants Condon and McGlaughlan were both in Grafton Dulany's company. Through the magic of bad paperwork, they suddenly appear here, with no explanation, in Costen's company. Most likely, it was part of the redistribution of Dulany's company after his death in December 1778.

Kelly had served with Walter Dulany's company for two years before being transferred just a short time prior to his desertion. Perhaps he didn't fancy his new company.

** What was it about March that made Philip Conden want to desert? After being reduced to private after his last escape attempt the previous March, he got it right this time. Watkins, formerly of Kennedy's company, was also no stranger to trouble. In September of 1778, he was a "prisoner in provost."

Name	Enlisted	Deserted
KENNEDY'S CO., JULY 14, 1781.		
Thomas Prust	6 Novr. 1777	29 April 1781
Martin Mealy [Melia]	1 April 1778	2 May 1781
John Powell	13 Novr. 1777	do*
John Kelly	6 Novr. 1777	5 May 1781
Henry Main	6 Novr. 1777	6 May 1781
Peter O'Neil†	6 Novr. 1777	27 May 1781
KEY'S CO., JULY 14, 1781.		
Peter Cochran [Coughran]	17 March 1778	27 April 1781
William Nixon	do	do
James Kelly	18 March 1778	Drum'd out of the Garrison at Pensacola
Cpl George Perry		9 May 1781
WALTER DULANY'S CO., JULY 14, 1781.		
Joseph Coast	13 Novr. 1777	25 April 1781
Anthony Float	do	do
Thomas Williams	19 Novr. 1777	29 April 1781
FRISBY'S CO., JULY 14, 1781.		
William Alford‡		8 May 1781
FRISBY'S CO., OCTOBER 25, 1782.§		
James Lowe	22 March 1778	9 Octr. 1782
Daniel Jones	do	15 Octr. 1782
James Murra	26 March 1778	do
James Tindell	do	do
Bernard Foster	?	10 Octr. 1782
JONES'S CO., OCTOBER 25, 1782.		
James [John] Start	27 April 1778	9 Octr. 1782

---

* Ditto

† Everyone except O'Neil apparently was trying to get out before the fort fell to the Spanish. It's easy to imagine that veterans Prust, Powell, Kelly, and Main (who had all joined at the same time and served three and a half years with the unit) saw what was coming and decided they'd had enough.

‡ William Alford is a mystery—absent from earlier muster rolls, he seems to pop up here out of nowhere.

§ Frisby's company may well be the worst-documented in the regiment. Many returns seem to be absent only in this company.

Name	Enlisted	Deserted
Darby Riggan [Derby Riggins]	1 May 1778	do
Thomas Pettit	1 March 1778	15 do
Nathaniel Leiger [Leger or Luger]	1 April 1778	do*
Joshua Townsend	26 March 1778	do

CAPTAIN DANIEL DULANY ADDISON'S CO., OCTOBER 25, 1782.

Cpl Ephraim Tilghman†	1 March 1778	9 Octr. 1782

KEY'S CO., DECEMBER 25, 1782.

John Henderson	3 Jany. 1778	3 Novr. 1782
Christian Smith [Smyth]	6 March 1778	24 do

KENNEDY'S CO., MARCH 5, 1783.

Thomas Gray	6 November 1777	24 Novr. 1782
Mark McNair	do	do

ADDISON'S CO., DECEMBER 25, 1782 – FEBRUARY 23, 1783.

Lewis Barcus‡	1 April 1778	24 Novr. 1782

KENNEDY'S CO., OCTOBER, 1783.

John Ratlif [Rutlif]	6 Novr. 1777	16 July 1783

KEY'S CO., OCTOBER, 1783.

John Stephens	6 Novr. 1777	16 July 1783

CAPTAIN JOHN STERLING'S CO., OCTOBER, 1783.

Richard Couple [Copple]§	10 April 1778	11 July 1783

Total: 154 documented desertions.

---

* Ditto

† The name Tilghman in Maryland is usually associated with Col. Tench Tilghman, the famous officer who served as Washington's aide-de-camp. Ephraim first shows up in Costen's company on July 11, 1778.

‡ The rolls show that George and Lewis Barcus joined W. Dulany's company on the same date.

§ Couple, also listed as Copple, has the honor of being the final documented deserter of the Maryland Loyalists. As he barely missed the opportunity of being shipwrecked, Mr. Couple was probably quite happy with his decision to quit when he did.

Maryland Loyalist Prisoners

The term "prisoner" can, of course, be extremely misleading. Some of these men were undoubtedly deserting to the other side. (Muster Rolls, National Archives of Canada, RG 8, "C" Series, Volumes 1904-1905)

Name	Enlisted	Taken Prisoner
G. Dulany's Co., July 11, 1778.		
Sgt. John Deighton	4 Decr. 1777	Taken Prisoner 18 June 1778
Costen's Co., July 11, 1778.		
Ensign John Cottman	31 May 1778	Taken Prisoner 18 June 1778 (with the rebels)
Jones's Co., September 4, 1778.		
Ensign Winder Cannon	28 March 1778	Prisoner (no date)
Robert Melvin	10 Decr. 1777	Taken Prisoner 3 Augt. 1778 (at Smith Town)
Key's Co., October 14, 1778.		
John Draper	27 April 1778	Prisoner (no date)
Kennedy's Co., United Corps Of Pennsylvania & Maryland Loyalists, April 24, 1780.		
Andrew Barber	4 Decr. 1777	Prisoner with ye Spaniards (no date)
W. Dulany's Co., April 25, 1780.		
Frederick Bechan	6 Novr. 1777	Taken Prisoner 24 Feby. 1780
James McQuire	?	Taken Prisoner 24 Feby. 1780
John Ratcliffe [Rutliff]	6 Novr. 1777	Taken Prisoner 24 Feby. 1780
John Sneichder [Schnider, Snider, Snither or Snyder]†	30 Novr. 1777	do*
William Wells	17 Feby. 1778	do

---

* Ditto

† It's a name like this that tortures genealogists. John S. (as I'll call him) sets the record for the most spellings of his name on the Maryland Loyalist muster rolls.

Name	Enlisted	Taken Prisoner
KENNEDY'S CO., JULY 14, 1781.		
James Cummins [Cummings]*	6 Novr. 1777	Prisoner with ye Spaniards [no date]
KEY'S CO., JULY 14, 1781.		
Patrick Harvey†		Prisoner with the Spaniards—Joined 17th April (1781)
W. DULANY'S CO., AUGUST 28, 1781.		
Thomas Clay‡	31 Decr. 1777	Prisoner with the Spaniards [no date]

MARYLAND LOYALISTS ON CAMPAIGN, JUNE–OCTOBER 1778

Captain Jones's orderly book listed the locations of the unit's encampments daily from June 18, 1778 (when they left Philadelphia with the British army) to October 12, 1778 (about the time they shipped out for Pensacola). The current names are in brackets.

June	18	Haddenfield [Haddonfield, New Jersey]
	20	Mores Town [Moorestown, New Jersey]
	20	Mount Holly
	22	Black Horse
	23	Camp at Cross Wicks [Crosswicks]
	24	Emelston [Emelstown]
	25	Freehold Township [near Monmouth Courthouse]
	28	Middleton [Middletown]
July	2	Camp [near Navesink]
	4	Camp [near Sandy Hook], New York

---

* Cummins returns from imprisonment on the 4/24/82 rolls.

† Harvey returns from Havanna on the 4/24/82 rolls (Maryland Historical Society, Rev. War Manuscripts, #MS 1814).

‡ It is of interest that Thomas Clay was listed on the 4/25/80 rolls as "Discharged, 24 Feby. 1780." Frederick Bechan, John Ratcliffe, William Wells, Thomas Clay, James Cummins, and Patrick Harvey were listed as "lately returned from Havana," 24 June 1782.

July	5	Sandy Hook
	7	Gravesend Bay
	14	Durryees House, Long Island
	30	Camp Jericho, Long Island
	31	Huntington, Long Island
Aug.	2	Smyths Town [Smithtown, Long Island]
	4	Satuckett [Setauket, Long Island]
	7	Weiden [Wading] River, Long Island
	8	Matituck [Mattituck, Long Island]
	10	Matituckett, Long Island
	25	Waiden [Wading] River [near Riverhead, Long Island]
	26	Miller's Place [Brookhaven, Long Island]
	28	Satuckett [Setauket, Long Island]
	30	Smyth Town
Sept	1	Huntington, Long Island
	3	Witberry, Long Island
	4	Flushing Fly, Long Island
Oct.	12	Flushing Fly, Long Island

Maryland Loyalist Commissioned Officers

The exact dates of officers' commissions quite often changed with each and every muster roll. Consequently, when only the month is given, multiple dates exist for that officer's commission. Comments: In the first paperwork of the regiment in October 1777, Ensigns William Ford and Thomas Hammond as well as Captains Ross Currie and Joseph Garnett appeared. All resigned shortly thereafter. Ross Currie later showed up as a lieutenant with the Pennsylvania Loyalists at Pensacola. (National Archives of Canada, Muster Rolls. Volumes 1904-1905; compiled by the author.)

Name and Rank	Commission	Notes
Lt. Col. James Chalmers	14 Oct 1777	
Maj. Walter Dulany	Nov. 1781	

Appendix

Name and Rank	Commission	Notes
Maj. John McDonald	11 Nov. 1777	Retired 30 Nov 1781
Chaplain John Patterson	1778	
Surgeon William Houston	1778	
Surgeon Alexander Kidd		Died 21 Nov 1778
Surgeon William Sinclair	Nov. 1777	
Surgeon William Stafford		
QM Joseph Garnett	Nov. 1777	
QM Thomas Walsh [Welch]	25 Oct 1778	
Adj. James Henley	0 Dec 1781	
Adj. James Miller	26 Oct 1778	
Capt Danial Dulany Addison	30 Nov 1781	
Capt Isaac Costen	29 May 1778	
Capt Grafton Dulany	Nov 1777	Died 23 Dec 1778
Capt Walter Dulany	10 Feb 1778	
Capt James Frisby	1777	Resigned Spring 1783
Capt Caleb Jones	25 Dec 1777	
Capt Patrick Kennedy	Oct/Nov 1777	
Capt Philip Barton Key	1 Mar 1778	
Capt Alexander Middleton	27 Oct 1777	Retired 1777
Capt John Sterling	16 Jul 1783	
Capt Levin Townsend	16 Jul 1783	
Lt John Boswell	27 Nov 1777	Resigned 1778
Lt Thomas Boswell	27 Nov 1777	
Lt Walter Dulany	1777	
Lt Thomas Gill	30 Jul 1783	
Lt James Henley	13 Mar 1783	
Lt James Inglis	27 Oct 1777	
Lt Philip Barton Key	1777	
Lt James Miller	26 Oct 1777	
Lt Thomas H. Parker	1 May 1778	Resigned 30 Oct 1778
Lt James Sinclair [St. Clair]	10 Feb 1778	
Lt John Sterling	1778	
Lt Willliam Sterling	12 Mar 1783	Died at sea 23-24 Sept, 1783
Lt Levin Townsend	1 May 1778	
Ensign Adam Allan	14 Oct 1777	
Ensign William A. Bowles	June 1778(?)	
Ensign Winder Cannon	Mar/May 1778	Prisoner 4 Sept 1778
Ensign John Chalmers	Aug 1783 (?)	
Ensign John Cottnam	29/31 May 1778	

Name and Rank	Commission	Notes
Ensign Thomas Gill	30/31 Jul 1783	
Ensign James Henley	Oct 1777	
Ensign William Jones	1 May 1778	Dead 24 Decr 1781
Ensign William Munro	31 May 1778	Resigned 24 Oct 1781
Ensign John McPherson	Nov 1777	
Ensign William Sterling [Stirling]	1778?	
Ensign John Stewart [Stuart]	Oct 1781	
Ensign Levin Vaughan	30/31 Jul 1783	Died at sea 23-24 Sept, 1783

Maryland Loyalists in New Brunswick

This list of Maryland Loyalist soldiers who settled in New Brunswick is the result of extensive cross-checking of other lists. Faulty records from the time have, no doubt, brought about errors. (Wright's *Loyalists of New Brunswick*; Muster Rolls, National Archives of Canada.)

KEY
BL. 1: Block 1, St. Ann [Fredericton]
BEL.: Belleisle, Kings County
BH: Beaver Harbour, Charlotte County
CARL.: Carleton County
GN.: Gagetown
KN.: Kingston, Kings County
MAUG.: Maugerville, Sunbury County
NASH.: Nashwaak, York County
P + Lot #: Parrtown (Saint John)
SCH.: Schoodic (St. Stephen), Charlotte County
UC: Upper Canada (Ontario)

Name	First Grant, Grant #	Subsequent Grant
Daniel Dulany Addison's Company		
William Morris	BL. 1 (#29)	
Ensign John Stewart, tailor [of Somerset County]	BL. 1 (#9)	

Appendix

Name	First Grant, Grant #	Subsequent Grant
Frisby's Company		
Fis[c]her, Barbara, Widow of John	BL. 1 (#35)	
Nehemiah Hayman	BL. 1 (#36)	
Kennedy's Company		
Nicholas Brock	BL. 1 (sold #43)	
Joseph Carroll, saddler	BL. 1 (#18)	
James Cummin[g]s	BL. 1 (#47)	
John Dunbar	SCH.	
Ensign Thomas Gill [of Delaware]	BL. 1 (#11)	
Simon Humphrey[s]	BL. 1 (#44)	
Captain Patrick Kennedy	P83/NASH.	Ireland
Drummer Robert Kerr [Carr]	BL. 1 (#42)	
James McDonald	BL. 1 (#48)	
Fergus McLeod	BL. 1 (#46)	
Cpl. Cannon Riggin [of Somerset County]	BL. 1 (#15)	
Sgt. Jacob Rogers	BL. 1 (#3)	
John Urquhart	BL. 1 (sold #5)	BEL.
Qt. Mstr. Thomas Walsh [Welch]	BL. 1 (#49)/NASH.	UC
Key's Company		
William Baynard	MAUG.	
Sgt. Lemuel Cohee	BL. 1 (#22)	
Lt. James Henley	P217	BL. 1 (#19,#50)
Cpl. William Savage, carpenter	BL. 1 (#17)	
John Shaddock	BL. 1 (#22)	
William Wells	BH	
Joseph White	BL. 1 (#45)	GN.
Samuel Woodward [Woodworth]	P221	BL. 1 (#24)
Thomas Young	P221	BL. 1 (#40)
Jones's Company		
Sgt. Zachariah Bailey	BL. 1 (#7)	

Name	First Grant, Grant #	Subsequent Grant
Drummer John Clements [Clemons]	BL. 1 (#39)	
Sgt. Robert Harris	BL. 1 (#23)	
Captain Caleb Jones [of Somerset County]	P211	BL. 1 (#37)
Cpl. James Love	P218	BL. 1 (#32)
George Matthews, mariner	BL. 1 (#30)	
Cpl. John Noble	BL. 1 (#32)	
Thomas Steeples	BL. 1 (#34)	
Henry White	BL. 1 (#31)/P220	NASH.

CAPTAIN JOHN STERLING'S COMPANY

Name	First Grant, Grant #	Subsequent Grant
Benjamin Butler, tailor	BL. 1 (#14)	
Joseph [John] Cayton	BL. 1 (#25)	
Cpl. Ephraim Cottingham	BL. 1 (#27)	
Isaac Harris	BL. 1 (#21)	
Hugh McDonald	BL. 1 (#26)	
Captain John Sterling [of Somerset County]	P216	BL. 1 (#10)

TOWNSEND'S COMPANY

Name	First Grant, Grant #	Subsequent Grant
Drummer Dennis Calla[g]han		
Daniel Fukes	BL. 1 (#1)	
Allen Morrison	BL. 1 (#2)	
Cpl. James McCo[o]mb	BL. 1 (#4)/NASH.	YORK CO.
Daniel McEvoy [McAvoy]	BL. 1 (#16)	CARL.?
Joseph Tallent [Fallent]	BL. 1 (#6)	KN.

Total: 48

Notes

CHAPTER 1

1. Algeo. "The Effects of the Revolution on Language," *Blackwell Encyclopedia of the American Revolution.* 592.
2. Lorenzo Sabine. *American Loyalists of the American Revolution*, I. 395.
3. Peter S. Onuf. *Maryland and the Empire*, 1773. 13.
4. Bernard Bailyn. *Ideological Origins of the American Revolution.* 91.
5. Force. *American Archives*, IV, v. IV. 714.
6. *Letters of Rev. Jonathan Boucher.* 184.
7. Bailyn. *Ideological Origins.* 315.
8. *Letters of Rev. Jonathan Boucher.* 184.
9. Charles J. Truitt. *Breadbasket of the Revolution.* 112.
10. *Ibid.* 112.
11. Bernard C. Steiner. *New Light on Some Maryland Loyalists.* 136.
12. Janet Bassett Johnson. *Robert Alexander, Maryland Loyalist.* 79.
13. *Ibid.* 81.
14. Truitt. 14.
15. Force. *American Archives*, III. 1574.
16. *Ibid.* 1571-76, 1582, 1585.
17. Oliver. *Journal of Samuel Curwen, Loyalist*, I. 116.

Chapter 2

1. Audit Office 12/6, 32-37.
2. *The Gentleman's Magazine,* Oct. 1806. 986.
3. John W. Jackson. *With the British Army in Philadelphia.* 104.
4. James Chalmers. *Plain Truth.* 5-6.
5. *Ibid.* 11.
6. Bernard Bailyn. *Ideological Origins of the American Revolution.* 288-89.
7. Cappon. *The Adams–Jefferson Letters.* 542. Adams to Jefferson, June 22, 1819.
8. Chalmers. *Plain Truth.* 16-17.
9. *Ibid.* 22.
10. Audit Office 12/6, 32-37.
11. James Chalmers. *Additions to Plain Truth.* 110-12.
12. Selwyn H. H. Carrington. "The American Revolution and the Sugar Colonies," Green. *Blackwell Encyclopedia of the American Revolution.* 508-17.
13. Chalmers. *Plain Truth.* 27.
14. *Ibid.* 29-30.
15. *Ibid.* 36.
16. Chalmers. *Additions to Plain Truth.* 103-4.
17. *Ibid.* 105.
18. *Ibid.* 130.
19. *Ibid.* 126.
20. *Ibid.* 122.
21. "Cato." "To the People of Pennsylvania, Letter III." *Pennsylvania Ledger,* Mar. 23, 1776. 1.
22. Oliver. *The Journal of Samuel Curwen, Loyalist,* I. 167.

Chapter 3

1. William Hand Browne. *Archives of Maryland,* XVI. 257.
2. Audit Office 12/6, 29-46.

3. Charles J. Truitt. *Breadbasket of the Revolution*. 166.
4. Browne. *Archives*, XVI. 122-23.
5. *Ibid*. 175-76.
6. *Ibid*. 196.
7. Audit Office 12/6, 29-46.
8. John Montresor. *Journals of Capt. John Montresor*. 440-41.
9. Browne. *Archives*, XVI. 339.
10. *Ibid*. 364.
11. Maryland State Papers. Red Book XXV, #28, Wilmer to Johnson, 07/28/1779, MSA S 989 MdHR 4593-32.
12. *Ibid*.
13. Browne. *Archives*, XXI. 486.
14. Browne. *Archives*, XVI. 409.
15. Janet Bassett Johnson. *Robert Alexander, Maryland Loyalist*. 104.
16. *Ibid*. 105.
17. Montresor. *Journals of Capt. John Montresor*. 442.
18. John André. *Major André's Journal*. 39.
19. Browne. *Archives*, XVI. 349.
20. Audit Office 12/6, 29-46.
21. Browne. *Archives*, XVI. 353.
22. *Pennyslvania Ledger*. 10/15/1777.
23. Thomas Hughes. *A Journal by Thomas Hughes*. 78.
24. Lorenzo Sabine. *Loyalists of the American Revolution*, I. 157.
25. *Ibid*. 597.
26. Audit Office 13/31/530-91.
27. *Royal Commission on the losses and services of American Loyalists*. . . . 387.
28. *Ibid*. 388.
29. Truitt. *Breadbasket*. 94.
30. Richard Arthur Overfield. *The Loyalists of Maryland during the American Revolution*. 220.
31. Browne. *Archives*, XVI. 241.
32. British Headquarters Papers, V. 5, No. 1311, Microfilm #742.
33. *The Carleton Sentinel*. Sept. 17, 1850.

34. Paul Leicester Ford, ed. *The Orderly Book of the Maryland Loyalist Regiment.* 7.

Chapter 4

1. John S. Jackson. *With the British Army in Philadelphia.* 152.
2. Pattison's order, *Ibid.* 174.
3. *Ibid.* 104.
4. Howe's orders quoted in the *Kemble Papers.* 527.
5. *Ibid.* 582.
6. *Ibid.*
7. British Headquarters Papers, V. 38, No. 94, Microfilm #10112.
8. William Hand Browne. *Archives of Maryland*, XVI. 485-86.
9. *Ibid.* 509.
10. Lorenzo Sabine. *Loyalists of the American Revolution*, I. 159.
11. *Kemble Papers.* 577.
12. Jackson. *With the British Army.* 266.
13. Paul Leicester Ford, ed. *Orderly Book of the Maryland Loyalists Regiment.* 15.
14. Public Archives of Canada, Ottawa. Maryland Loyalist Muster Rolls, Vols. 1904-1905.
15. *Simes' Military Medley.* Military terms.
16. Ford. *Orderly Book.* 27.
17. *Ibid.* 30-31.
18. Public Archives of Canada. Maryland Loyalist Muster Rolls, Vols. 1904-1905.
19. Ford. *Orderly Book.* 33-34.
20. *Ibid.* 38.
21. *Ibid.* 48.
22. *Ibid.* 51.
23. *Ibid.* 82.
24. *Ibid.* 56.
25. *Ibid.* 73.

26. William L. Clements Library. Sir Henry Clinton Papers. Chalmers to Clinton, Oct. 27, 1778.

Chapter 5

1. William L. Clements Library. Sir Henry Clinton Papers. Chalmers to Howe, Sept. 28, 1777.
2. *Ibid.*
3. *Ibid.* Chalmers to Clinton, July 24, 1778.
4. *Ibid.* Chalmers to Clinton, Sept. 12, 1778.
5. *Ibid.* Chalmers to Clinton, undated, 1778.
6. *Ibid.* Chalmers to Clinton, Sept. 12, 1778.
7. *Ibid.*
8. *Ibid.*
9. *Ibid.*
10. Public Record Office. British Headquarters Papers, Vol. 13, No. 55, Microfilm #2190.
11. William L. Clements Library. Clinton Papers. Chalmers to Clinton, July 26, 1779.
12. *Ibid.*
13. Thomas Hughes. *A Journal by Thomas Hughes.* 83.
14. William L. Clements Library. Clinton Papers. Chalmers to Clinton, July 26, 1779.
15. *Ibid.*
16. *Ibid.*
17. *Ibid.*
18. *Ibid.*
19. *Ibid.* Chalmers to André, Apr. 26, 1780.
20. Public Record Office. British Headquarters Papers, Vol. 20, No. 189, Microfilm #2983.
21. William L. Clements Library. Clinton Papers. Chalmers to Clinton, July 21, 1780.
22. *Ibid.* Chalmers to Clinton, October 13, 1780.

23. *Ibid.*
24. Lt.-Gen. Earl Cornwallis. *An Answer to that part of the Narrative af Lieutenant-General Sir Henry Clinton.* 98-99.
25. *Ibid.* 99.

Chapter 6

1. William L. Clements Library. Clinton Papers. Chalmers to Lord Rawdon, May 21, 1779.
2. J. Barton Starr. *Tories, Dons & Rebels.* 130.
3. Public Archives of Canada, Ottawa. Raymond, ed. *Edward Winslow Papers.* 40.
4. National Archives of Canada. Maryland Loyalist Muster Rolls, Vols. 1904-1905.
5. Starr. *Tories, Dons & Rebels.* 132.
6. *Ibid.*
7. National Archives of Canada. Maryland Loyalist Muster Rolls, Vols. 1904-1905.
8. Starr. *Tories, Dons & Rebels.* 134.
9. J. Leitch Wright, Jr. *William Augustus Bowles, Director General of the Creek Nation.* 12-13.
10. Raymond, ed. *Winslow Papers.* 46.
11. Public Record Office. British Headquarters Papers, Vol. 13, No. 55, Microfilm #2190.
12. William L. Clements Library. Clinton Papers. Chalmers to Lord Rawdon, May 21, 1779.
13. Public Record Office. British Headquarters Papers, Microfilm #2736.
14. National Archives of Canada. *Winslow Papers*, Reel 1, Document 145.
15. Starr. *Tories, Dons & Rebels.* 183.
16. *Ibid.*
17. J. Leitch Wright, Jr. *William Augustus Bowles.* 14.

18. Robert Farmar. "Bernardo de Galvez's Siege of *Pensacola*," Vol. 26, No. 2, April 1943 (reprint). 10.
19. Winston De Ville, ed. *Yo Solo, The Battle Journal of Bernardo de Galvez during the American Revolution*. 16.
20. *Ibid*. 18.
21. Lorenzo Sabine. *Loyalists of the American Revolution*, I. 245.
22. De Ville. *Yo Solo*. 20.
23. Farmar. "Bernardo de Galvez's Siege." 17.
24. De Ville. *Yo Solo*. 27.
25. Farmar. "Bernardo de Galvez's Siege." 16.
26. N. Orwin Rush. *The Battle of Pensacola*. 107.
27. *The Carleton Sentinel and Family Journal*. "Reward of a Venerable Amazon." September 17, 1850.
28. De Ville. *Yo Solo*. 31.
29. Starr. *Tories, Dons & Rebels*. 214.
30. National Archives of Canada. Maryland Loyalist Muster Rolls, Vols. 1904-1905. Regimental returns, October 25- December 24, 1781.
31. Memorial of Philip Barton Key, June 22, 1785, *Royal Commission on the losses and services of American Loyalists*. 387.
32. Wright. *William Augustus Bowles*. 17.

Chapter 7

1. Claude Halstead Van Tyne. *Loyalists in the American Revolution*. 297.
2. *Ibid*. 296-97.
3. Christopher Moore. *The Loyalists, Revolution, Exile, Settlement*. 149.
4. Public Record Office. British Headquarters Papers, Vol. 38, No. 94, Microfilm #10112; Vol. 38, No. 94, Microfilm #7784.
5. Kennedy's Journal as quoted in Raymond, *Winslow Papers*. 138.
6. *Ibid*.
7. Lorenzo Sabine. *Loyalists of the American Revolution*, I. 530.

8. *Carleton Sentinel and Family Journal.* Sept. 17, 1850.
9. Raymond, ed. *Winslow Papers.* 138.
10. *Nova-Scotia Gazette.* Oct. 28, 1783.
11. Moore. *The Loyalists.* 183.
12. Sabine. *Loyalists,* II. 26.
13. Marion Gilroy. *Loyalists and Land Settlement in Nova Scotia.* 146.
14. *Ibid.* 148.
15. Esther Clark Wright. *Loyalists of New Brunswick.* 220.
16. *Ibid.* 241.
17. Moore. *The Loyalists.* 200.
18. Raymond, ed. *Winslow Papers.* 284.
19. Esther Clark Wright. *The Saint John River.* 185.
20. *Ibid.* 159.
21. Raymond, ed. *Winslow Papers.* 211.
22. Wright. *Loyalists of New Brunswick.* 181.
23. *Carleton Sentinel.* Sept. 17, 1850.
24. Maryland State Papers. Red Book XXIX, #28, Stevenson to Brice, 05/02/1782 MSA S 898 MdHR 4591-31.
25. Public Record Office. British Headquarters Papers, Vol. 52, No. 119, Microfilm #7243.
26. *Ibid.*
27. Sabine. *Loyalists,* I. 397.
28. Richard Arthur Overfield. *The Loyalists of Maryland during the American Revolution.* 420.

Chapter 8

1. J. Leitch Wright. *William Augustus Bowles.* 20.
2. *Ibid.* 22.
3. *Ibid.* 64.
4. *Ibid.* 133

5. *Ibid.* 171.
6. Victor Weybright. *Spangled Banner.* 178.
7. *Ibid.* 43.
8. *Ibid.* 20.
9. *Ibid.* 20.
10. *Ibid.* 221.
11. *Ibid.* 177.
12. Janet Bassett Johnson. *Robert Alexander, Maryland Loyalist.* 115.
13. *Ibid.* 116.
14. *Ibid.* 117.
15. Public Record Office. British Headquarters Papers. Audit Office 12/8, 117/59.
16. Johnson. *Robert Alexander.* 126-27.
17. Public Archives of Canada, Ottawa. *Edward Winslow Papers.* Reel 4, Document 79.
18. *Ibid.* Document 84.
19. Harriet Irving Library. Saunders Family Papers. Chalmers to Saunders, October 9, 1797.
20. *Ibid.* Chalmers to Saunders, June 5, 1792.
21. *Ibid.* Chalmers to Saunders, December 12, 1796.
22. Lt. Col. James Chalmers. *Strictures on a Pamphlet Written by Thomas Paine on the English System of Finance.* 2.
23. *Ibid.* 52.
24. *Ibid.* 60.
25. *Ibid.* 67.
26. *Ibid.* 65.
27. Harriet Irving Library. Saunders Family Papers. Chalmers to Saunders, July 15, 1797.
28. *The Gentleman's Magazine.* Nov. 1804. 1043.
29. Public Archives of Canada, Ottawa. *Edward Winslow Papers.* Reel 12, Vol. XVII, Document 66.
30. *The Gentleman's Magazine.* Oct. 1806. 986.
31. Harriet Irving Library. Saunders Family Papers. Saunders to Major Alexander Jekyll Chalmers, December 15, 1806.

Bibliography

Manuscripts

National Archives of Canada, Ottawa/David Library of the American Revolution (microfilm):
    Edward Winslow Papers, 1695-1877 (MG23 D2)
    Maryland Loyalist Muster Rolls, Vols. 1904-1905

William L. Clements Library, Ann Arbor, Michigan:
    Sir Henry Clinton Papers
    Addison Papers

Harriet Irving Library, University of New Brunswick:
    Saunders Family Papers/ Military Affairs/Archives and Special Collections

Public Record Office, London/David Library of the American Revolution (microfilm):
    British Headquarters (Guy Carleton) Papers
    Audit Office 12,13

Maryland State Archives, Annapolis:
    Red Books XXV, XXIX

Newspapers

The Carleton Sentinel and Family Journal. James S. Segee, publisher, 1850.

The Gentleman's Magazine. London: Nichols and Son, printers, 1783-1806.

The Nova-Scotia Gazette: and the Weekly Chronicle, 1783.

The Pennsylvania Ledger: Or the Virginia, Maryland, Pennsylvania, & New Jersey Weekly Advertiser. Philadelphia: James Humphreys, Jr., printer, 1775-1778.

Books

André, John. *Major André's Journal. Operations of the British Army under Lieutenant Generals Sir William Howe and Sir Henry Clinton, June 1777 to November 1778, recorded by Major André, Adjutant General.* New York: Arno Press, 1968 reprint.

Bailyn, Bernard. *Ideological Origins of the American Revolution.* Cambridge, Mass.: Harvard University Press, 1967.

Barker, Lt. John. *The British in Boston: Being the Diary of Lt. John Barker of the King's Own Regiment from Nov. 15, 1774 to May 31, 1776; with notes by Elizabeth Ellery Dana.* Cambridge, Mass.: Harvard University Press, 1924.

Billias, George Athan, ed. *George Washington's Opponents: British Generals & Admirals in the American Revolution.* New York: William Morrow & Co., 1969.

Boatner, Mark M. III. *Encyclopedia of the American Revolution.* Mechanicsburg, Pa.: Stackpole Books, 1966, 1994 reprint.

Botsford, Jay Barrett. *English Society in the Eighteenth Century as Influenced from Overseas.* New York: MacMillan Company, 1924.

Brown, Wallace. *The Good Americans: The Loyalists in the American Revolution.* New York: William Morrow & Co., 1969.

Browne, William Hand, ed. *Archives of Maryland XI, Journal of the Maryland Convention, July 26-August 14, 1775, Journal and Correspondence of the Maryland Council of Safety, August 29, 1775 to July 6, 1776.* Baltimore: Maryland Historical Society, 1892.

_____ *Archives of Maryland XVI, Journal and Correspondence of the Council of Safety, January 1-March 20, 1777, Journal and Correspondence of the State Council, March 20, 1777-March 28, 1778.* Baltimore: Maryland Historical Society, 1897.

_____ *Archives of Maryland XXI, Journal and Correspondence of the State Council, 1778-1779.* Baltimore: Maryland Historical Society, 1901.

Bunnell, Paul J. *Research Guide to Loyalist Ancestors: A Directory of Archives, Manuscripts, and Published Sources.* Bowie, Md.: Heritage Books, 1990.

Callahan, North. *Royal Raiders: The Tories of the American Revolution.* Indianapolis, Ind.: Bobbs-Merrill Company, 1963.

Cappon, Lester J., ed. *The Adams-Jefferson Letters: The Complete Correspondence between Thomas Jefferson and Abigail and John Adams.* Chapel Hill: University of North Carolina Press, 1959, 1988.

Cornwallis, Lieutenant-General Earl. *An Answer to that part of the Narrative of Lieutenant-General Sir Henry Clinton, K.B., Which relates to the Conduct of Lt. Gen. Earl Cornwallis during the Campaign in North America, in the year 1781.* New York: Research Reprints, 1970 reprint of 1783 original.

De Ville, Winston, ed. *Yo Solo: The Battle Journal of Bernardo De Galvez during the American Revolution.* New Orleans, La.: Polyanthos, 1978.

Egerton, Hugh Edward, ed. *The Royal Commission on the Losses and Services of American Loyalists,* 1783-1785. New York: Burt Franklin, 1971.

Ferling, John E. *The Loyalist Mind: Joseph Galloway and the American Revolution.* State College, Pa.: Pennsylvania State University Press, 1977.

Force, Peter, ed. *American Archives: Consisting of a Collection of Authentick Records, State Papers, Debates, and Letters and other Notices of Public Affairs. . . .* Fourth Series, 6 vols. Washington, D.C.: By the editor, 1837-1846.

Ford, Paul Leicester, ed. *Orderly Book of the Maryland Loyalists Regiment, June 18th, 1778 to October 12th, 1778.* Brooklyn, N.Y.: Historical Printing Club, 1891.

Gilroy, Marion. *Loyalists and Land Settlement in Nova Scotia.* Baltimore: Genealogical Publishing Co., 1990 reprint.

Green, Jack P., and J.R. Pole, eds. *Blackwell Encyclopedia of the American Revolution.* Oxford, England: Blackwell Publishers, 1991.

Hibbert, Christopher. *Redcoats and Rebels: The American Revolution through British Eyes.* New York: Avon Books, 1991.

Hughes, Thomas. *A Journal by Thomas Hughes (Ensign of the 53rd Regiment), For his Amusements, & Designed only for his Perusal by the time he attains the Age of 50 if he lives so long, 1778-1789.* Cambridge, England: Cambridge University Press, 1947.

Jackson, John W. *With the British Army in Philadelphia, 1777- 1778.* San Rafael, Calif.: Presidio Press, 1979.

Johnson, Janet Bassett. *Robert Alexander, Maryland Loyalist.* New York: G. P. Putnam's & Sons, 1942.

Kemble, Stephen. *Journals of Lieut.-Col. Stephen Kemble, 1773- 1789; and British Army Orders: Gen. Sir William Howe, 1775-1778; Gen. Sir Henry Clinton, 1778; and Gen. Daniel Jones, 1778.* Boston: Gregg Press, 1972 reprint.

Land, Aubrey C., ed. *Letters from America.* Cambridge, Mass.: Belknap Press of Harvard University Press, 1969.

Montresor, John. *Journals of Capt. John Montresor from the collections of the New-York Historical Society for the year 1881.* New York: New-York Historical Society, 1882.

Moore, Christopher. *The Loyalists, Revolution, Exile, Settlement.* Toronto, Canada: McCelland & Stewart, 1994.

Moore, Frank. *Diary of the American Revolution*. Vols. 1 and 2. New York: Charles T. Evans, 1863.

Moore, Frank. *Songs & Ballads of the American Revolution*. New York: D. Appleton & Co., 1856.

Nelson, William H. *The American Tory*. Boston: Northeastern University Press, 1992 reprint.

Oliver, Andrew, ed. *The Journal of Samuel Curwen, Loyalist*. Vols. 1 and 2. Cambridge, Mass.: Harvard University Press, 1972.

Onuf, Peter S., ed. *Maryland and the Empire, 1773, The Antilon-First Citizen Letters*. Baltimore: Johns Hopkins University Press, 1974.

Plumb, J. H. *The First Four Georges: England and Her "German" Kings, 1714-1830*. Boston: Little, Brown & Company, 1956.

Randall, Willard Sterne. *Benedict Arnold, Patriot and Traitor*. New York: Quill/William Morrow, 1990.

Raymond, William O., ed. *The Winslow Papers, A.D. 1776-1826*. Boston: Gregg Press, 1972 reprint.

Rush, N. Orwin. *The Battle of Pensacola*. Tallahassee: Florida State University Press, 1966.

Sabine, Lorenzo. *Loyalists of the American Revolution*. Baltimore: Genealogical Pub. Co., 1979 reprint of 2 volumes from the 1864 second edition.

Scheer, George F., and Hugh F. Rankin. *Rebels and Redcoats*. Cleveland, Ohio: World Publishing Company, 1957.

Siebert, Wilbur Henry. *The Loyalists of Pennsylvania*. Boston: Gregg Press, 1972 reprint.

Simes, Thomas. *The Military Medley: Containing the most necessary rules and directions for attaining a competent knowledge of the art: to which is added an explanation of military terms*. London: 1768, and Oldwick, N.J.: King's Arms Press, 1995 reprint.

Stark, James H. *The Loyalists of Massachusetts and the Other Side of the American Revolution*. Boston: W.B. Clarke Co., 1910, and Bowie, Md.: Heritage Books, 1988 reprint.

Starr, J. Barton. *Tories, Dons & Rebels: The American Revolution in British West Florida*. Gainesville: University Presses of Florida, 1976.

Truitt, Charles J. *Breadbasket of the Revolution: Delmarva's Eight Turbulent War Years*. Salisbury, Md.: Historical Books, 1975.

Van Tyne, Claude Halstead. *The Loyalists in the American Revolution*. New York: MacMillan Co., 1902, and Bowie, Md.: Heritage Books, 1989 reprint.

Weybright, Victor. *Spangled Banner*. New York: Farrar & Rinehart, 1935.

Wright, Esther Clark. *The Loyalists of New Brunswick*. Fredericton, N.B.: privately published, 1955.

Wright, Esther Clark. *The Saint John River*. Toronto: McClelland & Stewart, 1949.

Wright, J. Leitch, Jr. *William Augustus Bowles, Director General of the Creek Nation*. Athens: University of Georgia Press, 1967.

Pamphlets

Chalmers, James ("Candidus"). *Plain Truth; Addressed to the Inhabitants of America, Containing Remarks on a Late Pamplet entitled "Common Sense."* Philadelphia: Robert Bell, 1776.

Chalmers, James ("Candidus"). [Additions to] *Plain Truth; Addressed to the Inhabitants of America, Containing Further Remarks On a Late Pamplet entitled "Common Sense."* Philadelphia: Robert Bell, 1776.

Chalmers, Lieutenant-Colonel [James]. *Strictures on a Pamplet Written by Thomas Paine, on the English System of Finance: to which are added some remarks on the war, and other national concerns*. 2nd ed. London: J. Debrett, 1796.

Articles

"Letters of Reverend Jonathan Boucher." *Maryland Historical Magazine* 8 (March-December 1913): 168-86.

Farmar, Robert. "Bernardo de Galvez's Siege of Pensacola in 1781 (as Related in Robert Farmar's Journal)." Edited by James A. Padgett. *Louisiana Historical Quarterly*, vol. 26, no. 2 (April 1943): 311-29.

Jones, E. Alfred. "The Real Author of the 'Authentic Memoirs of William Augustus Bowles.'" *Maryland Historical Magazine*, vol. 18 (December 1923): 300-8.

New, M. Christopher. "Maryland Loyalists: The Forgotten People of the American Revolution." *Maryland Magazine*, May/June 1995: 36-41.

Papenfuse, Edward C., Jr. "Economic Analysis & Loyalist Strategy during the American Revolution: Robert Alexander's Remarks on the Economy of the Peninusula or Eastern Shore of Maryland." *Maryland Historical Magazine,* vol. 68, no. 2 (summer 1973): 175-85.

Parks, Virginia. "The British Fort at Pensacola." *Pensacola History Illustrated*, vol. 3, no. 4 (spring-summer 1990), 11-18.

Rea, Robert R. "British Pensacola." *Pensacola History Illustrated*, vol. 3, no. 4 (spring-summer 1990): 3-10.

Steiner, Henry F. "New Light on Some Maryland Loyalists," *Maryland Historical Magazine* vol. 2 (June 1907): 133-37.

Unpublished Sources

Overfield, Richard Arthur. *The Loyalists of Maryland during the American Revolution*. Dissertation: University of Maryland, 1968.

Index

Numbers in italic designate illustrations.

Adams, John, 24, 25, 34
Addison, Capt. Daniel Dulany, 102
Additions to Plain Truth, 21, 29-33, *30*, 68
Agnew, Capt. Stair, 126
Allen, Ens. Adam, 56
Allen, Rev. Bennet, 114
Allen, Lt. Col. William, 46, 56, 65, 84, 85
Alexander, Robert, 13-14, 41, 42, 67-68, 79, 123-25
    family of, 124-25
Andre, Maj. John, 40, 43, 56, 76-77, 97
Annapolis, Md., 4, 7, 11, 12, 39, 45, 47, 69, 72, 114, 121, 122
Antilon & First Citizen Letters, 6-9
Arnold, Benedict, 46, 76, 123, 132
Atkinson, Isaac, 15-16

Baltimore, Md., 4, 5, 13, 42, 48, 69-72, 79, 121
Bay of Fundy, Nova Scotia, 110
Bell, Robert, 20-21, 33, 52
Bladensburg, Md., 114
"Block 1," 109, 110
Boston, 11, 13, 15, 16, 27, 33, 58, 108
Boswell, Lt. John, 65

Boucher, Rev. Jonathan, 11-13
Bowles, William Augustus
    enlists in Md. Loyalists, 49
    resigns commission, 84
    rejoins regiment, 88
    dir. gen. of Creek Nation, 115-20
    death of, 120
Brown, Pvt. Peter, 64
Brown, Wallace, 10
Burgoyne, Gen. John, 45, 72

Calvert, George, 4
Campbell, Gen. John, 70, 81, 84-88, 90, 93, 94
Cannon, Ens. Winder, 86
Carleton, Guy, 100, 107, 113
Carroll, Charles, 6-9
"Cato," 33
Cecil Co., Md., 13, 43, 67, 124
Chalmers, Alexander Jekyll, 130
Chalmers, Lt. Col. James
    writes *Plain Truth*, 19-34
    commissioned lt. col., 46
    plan for Eastern Shore, 66-80
    contests rank at Pensacola, 85-86

Chalmers, Lt. Col. James *(cont.)*
   returns to army service, 129
   disagrees with Simcoe, 129
   writes *Strictures*, 127-29
   Ariana Margaretta (daughter), 126
   death of, 130
Chandler, Rev. Thomas, 11
Charleston, S.C., 71, 74, 76
Charlestown, Md., 70
Chase, Judge Jeremiah T., 121
Chase, Samuel, 14, 122
Chattahoochee River, Fla., 84
Chelsea, England, 129
Chester, Gov. Peter, 81
Chestertown, Md., 10, 15, 19, 20, 35, 39, 40, 124
"Chestertown Tea Party," 15
Chipman, Ward, 107, 131
Choptank River, Md., 69
Clifton, Lt. Col. Alfred, 45, 56
Clinton, Sir Henry, 56, 60, 65, 67-80, 82, 85, 86
Cockey, Thomas, 13
Common Sense, 18-34, 52
Cooper, Rev. Myles, 11
Cornwallis, Lt. Gen. Earl, 79, 80, 82, 95, 132
Costen, Isaac, 49, 55, 83-84, 86, 88
Creek Indians, 84, 116-20
Curwen, Samuel, 17, 33

Danbury, Conn., 61
DeLancey's Brigade, 101, 104-5, 131
Dickinson, John, 14, 21-24
Dulany, Daniel, 6-9
   Capt. Grafton, 83
   Lloyd, 114
   Capt. Walter, 95, 98, 113-14, 126

Eden, Gov. Robert, 7, 8, 20, 114
Edmondston, Rev. William, 13
Emelstown, N.J., 58
Erskine, Sir William, 60, 77

Fanning, Lt. Col. Edmund, 126-27
Federal Gazette, 123
France, 5, 25-26, 27-28, 68, 73, 82, 96, 127, 129
Franklin, William, 46, 125, 130
Frederick, Md., 49, 120, 121
Fredericton, New Brunswick, 126, 129
Freehold, N.J., 59-60
Frisby, Capt. James, 40, 64, 72, 88, 96, 100

Gage Hill, Pensacola, 87
Galloway, Joseph, 44, 46, 52, 68
Galvez, Bernardo de, 87-92
Geddes, 15
George III, King, 26, 72, 82
Germaine, Lord George, 56
Germantown, Battle of, 43
   Howe's headquarters at, 45
Gordon, Hugh Mackay, 83, 85, 86
Gravesend, Long Island, 60

Haddonfield, N.J., 57
Hancock, John, 37
Head of Elk (Elkton), 13, *38*, 39, 40, 41, 42, 43, 68, 70, 123
Heath, Daniel, 40
Henley, Lt. James, 102, 104
"Herimitage, The," 124
Hollingsworth, Jesse, 42
Hopkins, Jeremiah, 110

Howe, Sir William, 34, 37, 41-46, 50, 55-57, 65-68, 73, 76
Hughes, Ens. Thomas, 72
Huntington, Long Island, 61, 67

Jefferson, Thomas, 34, 119, 122
Johnson, Gov. Thomas, 37, 39, 43, 45
Jones, Capt. Caleb, 49, 55, 57, 58, 60, 63, 64, 84, 101, 110, 112

Kearsley, John, 47
Kennedy, Capt. Patrick, 48-49, 84, 89, 101, 102, 104-5, 109-10
Kent Co., Md., 11, 19, 26, 35, 40, 43, 67, 72, 74, 125, 129
Key, Francis Scott, 47, 120-22
Key, John Ross, 47, 121
Key, Capt. Philip Barton, 47-48, 55, 88, 96, 100, 101, 120-23
Kuyphausen, Gen. Wilhelm, 58

Lancaster, Pa., 45, 73, 79
Leonardtown, Md., 121
Lexington/Concord, Battle of, 9, 18
Louis XVI, King, 28

MacDonald, Maj. John, 49, 92-93
Mackenzie, Frederick, 113
Marshall, Chief Justice John, 123
Martha, sinking of the, 102-5
Maryland Council of Safety, 13, 14, 15, 16, 36
Maryland Loyalists, First Batt. of
   commission of, 45
   officers in, 46-49
   desertions in, 58, 63-64, 90-91, 93, 95
   soldiers disciplined, 64
   British attitude toward, 84
   in bayonet attacks, 92-93
   land grants of, 109-13
Maryland State Council, 35, 39, 40, 48, 55, 78, 123
Mathew, Gen. Edward, 74-75
Mattituck, Long Island, 63
McPherson, Ens. John, 55
Meschianza, 56-57
Middleton, Capt. Alexander, 46-47, 56
Middletown, N.J., 59
Miller, Lt. James, 86
Mobile, attack on, 88
Monmouth, Battle of, 59-60
Montresor, Capt. John, 37, 39, 41-43, 45, 56, 66
Moorestown, N.J., 58
Moro Castle, Havana, 119-20
Murray, (Earl of Dunmore) John, 116

Nashwaak River, New Brunswick, 126
Nassau, Bahamas, 116
New Castle, Del., 126
New Jersey Gazette, 63
New Jersey Volunteers, 58
Newtown. *See* Chestertown
Nanticoke Indians, 5

Odell, Rev. Jonathan, 46
Oliver Wiswell, 131
Osborne's Hotel, London, 116
Oxford, Md., 69, 79

Paca, William, 14, 39-40, 43, 124
Paine, Thomas, 18-31, 127

Parker, Lt. Thomas, 65
Paterson, Rev. John, 10-11, 39-40, 49
Pennyslvania Loyalists, First Batt. of, 45-46, 50, 56, 84, 93-94
Pensacola, Fla., 82-95
  fortification of, 87
  battle of, 91, *92*, 93-95
  surrender of, 94-95
Perkins, Isaac "Colonel," 35-36
Philadelphia, 11, 14, 18, 20-21, 32, 37, 39, 40, 43-57, 62, 66, 69, 75, 97, 118
Plain Truth, 18-34, 22, *23*, *30*, 67, 68, 127, 129
  France's involvement, 27-28
  on the British Constitution, 24
  on democracy, 24-25
Port au Prince, Haiti, 129
Prince Edward Island, Canada, 126-27

Queen's Rangers, 56, 118, 126

Randolph, John, 123
Rawdon, Lord, 76, 85
Ridgely, Charles, 13
Rivington's Royal Gazette, 46, 100
Roberts, Kenneth, 131
Roman Catholic Volunteers, 45-46, 55, 59, 62
Ryan's Theater Co., Dennis, 115

Sabine, Lorenzo, 91
St. Anne's. *See* Fredericton
St. Augustine, Fla., 82
St. Domingo, 130
Saint John, 100, 105, 107, 108, 115
St. John's College, Annapolis, 121
St. Mark's, Fla., 118-19

Saratoga, surrender at, 45, 72
Saunders, John, 126-27, 129, 131
Savannah, Ga., 71
Setauket, Long Island, 62
Sharpe, Gov. Horatio, 5
Shelburne, Nova Scotia, 106
Simcoe, Col. John, 79, 118, 129
Slubey, William, 39-40, 78
Smallwood, Brig. Gen. William, 36-37, 45
Smithtown, Long Island, 62
Snow Hill, Md., 36
Somerset, HMS, 40
Somerset County, Md., 15-16, 49
Southwark Theatre, Philadelphia, 53
Stafford, Surgeon William, 104, 131
"Star Spangled Banner," 121
Sterling, Capt. John, 48, 55, 64, 100, 101
  Isaac, 48, 55
  Henry, 48
  William, 48, 104
Strictures..., 127, *128*, 129
Susquehonnock Indians, 5

Tecumseh, 120
Tilghman, Matthew, 13
Townsend, Levin, 15, 49, 55, 101
Tryon, Maj. Gen. William, 61, 62, 63

Upton House, England, 131

Vaughan, Gen. John, 45

Waldeck Regiment, 83, 88, 92, 93

Washington, city of, 122-23
Washington, George, 11, 14, 32, 37, 41, 43, 52, 54, 57-58, 59, 69, 70, 74, 76, 77, 95, 115, 118, 132
West Indies, British, 19, 26-27, 76, 129, 130
Williamsburg, Va., 70
Wilmer, Rev. James Josias, 18, 40
Wilson, James, 14

Winslow, Edward, 82-83, 85, 86, 109, 110, 125-26, 130, 131
Woodley Mansion, 123
Woodward, Elizabeth, 49-50, 94, 101, 104, 110-11
  Samuel, 49, 94, 104

Yarmouth, Nova Scotia, 104
Yorktown, surrender at, 80, 95, 96, 124